"R.J. Patterson does a fantastic job at keeping you engaged and interested. I look forward to more from this talented author."

- Aaron Patterson
bestselling author of SWEET DREAMS

DEAD SHOT

"Small town life in southern Idaho might seem quaint and idyllic to some. But when local newspaper reporter Cal Murphy begins to un-cover a series of strange deaths that are linked to a sticky spider web of deception, the lid on the peaceful town is blown wide open. Told with all the energy and bravado of an old pro, first-timer R.J. Patterson hits one out of the park his first time at bat with *Dead Shot*. It's that good."

- Vincent Zandri
bestselling author of THE REMAINS

"You can tell R.J. knows what it's like to live in the newspaper world, but with *Dead Shot*, he's proven that he also can write one heck of a murder mystery."

- Josh Katzowitz
NFL writer for CBSSports.com
& author of Sid Gillman: Father of the Passing Game

"Patterson has a mean streak about a mile wide and puts his two main characters through quite a horrible ride, which makes for good reading."

- Richard D., reader

DEAD LINE

"This book kept me on the edge of my seat the whole time. I didn't really want to put it down. R.J. Patterson has hooked me. I'll be back for more."

- Bob Behler
3-time Idaho broadcaster of the year
and play-by-play voice for Boise State football

"Like a John Grisham novel, from the very start I was pulled right into the story and couldn't put the book down. It was as if I personally knew and cared about what happened to each of the main characters. Every chapter ended with so much excitement and suspense I had to continue to read until I learned how it ended, even though it kept me up until 3:00 A.M.

- Ray F., reader

DEAD IN THE WATER

"In Dead in the Water, R.J. Patterson accurately captures the action-packed saga of a what could be a real-life college football scandal. The sordid details will leave readers flipping through the pages as fast as a hurry-up offense."

- Mark Schlabach,
ESPN college sports columnist and
co-author of *Called to Coach*
and *Heisman: The Man Behind the Trophy*

THE WARREN OMISSIONS

"What can be more fascinating than a super high concept novel that reopens the conspiracy behind the JFK assassination while the threat of a global world war rests in the balance? With his new novel, *The Warren Omissions*, former journalist turned bestselling author R.J. Patterson proves he just might be the next worthy successor to Vince Flynn."

- Vincent Zandri
bestselling author of THE REMAINS

OTHER TITLES BY R.J. PATTERSON

Cal Murphy Thrillers
Dead Shot
Dead Line
Better off Dead
Dead in the Water
Dead Man's Curve
Dead and Gone
Dead Wrong
Dead Man's Land
Dead Drop
Dead to Rights
Dead End

James Flynn Thrillers
The Warren Omissions
Imminent Threat
The Cooper Affair
Seeds of War

Brady Hawk Thrillers
First Strike
Deep Cover
Point of Impact
Full Blast
Target Zero
Fury
State of Play
Siege
Seek and Destroy
Into the Shadows
Hard Target
No Way Out
Two Minutes to Midnight
Against All Odds
Amy Means Necessary
Vengeance
Code Red

VENGEANCE

A Brady Hawk novel

R.J. PATTERSON

VENGEANCE
© Copyright 2018 R.J. Patterson

First Print Edition 2019

Cover Design by Books Covered

Published in the United States of America
Green E-Books
Boise Idaho 83713

*For Chad, a great soldier
and a great American*

CHAPTER 1

Nuba Mountains, Sudan

WISPS OF DUST settled onto Brady Hawk's lips as he peered through his binoculars at the target location below in a small ravine. Despite the milder December temperatures, Hawk's mouth was still dry from nestling beneath a blind on the sandy ground. Sweat beaded on his forehead with the occasional drop breaking loose and streaking down his face. But for all his discomfort, staking out an enemy combatant allowed Hawk an opportunity to think about something else, anything else than the one painful memory that had dominated his thoughts for the past six months.

Losing his mother was difficult enough, but the brutal manner in which she was murdered stoked Hawk's determination to hunt down the animal who'd killed her and repay them. There was only one problem: there wasn't a single clue local law enforcement had gathered from the scene. Not a piece of fabric, not a strand of hair, not a drop of blood. Whoever murdered her not only was a professional but one of the best the Dallas Police Department had ever encountered. According to their initial and subsequent reports, the killer was highly trained and skilled. And with as much time passing as it had, Hawk was confident the case had already been relegated to the growing mountain of unsolved murders in the cold case files.

But the mission to Sudan was a welcome distraction to the numbing pain. Hawk also had a place to focus his ire until he learned the identity of his mother's killer.

Hawk was accompanied by Titus Black, both men perched on opposing ridges about fifty meters above the valley floor, only a short sprint down the hill if their mission required it. But Hawk hoped this would be an easy mission—two shots and vanish into the wind.

Hawk had been in place for nearly two hours with barely a word uttered over his coms to either Alex or Black. There wasn't much to say until the alleged meeting commenced.

The Phoenix Foundation had been closely monitoring the reemergence of Al Hasib, now called Al Fatihin under the direction of Evana Bahar. As

Bahar used her fundraising expertise learned while leading a non-profit in London, she ran into problems moving funds through various banking systems. She wasn't prepared for the constant freezing of her accounts or outright removal of small fortunes. Her attempt to correct this nagging issue was to contact South African diamond launderer Freddie Jacobs.

Jacobs was on scores of terrorist watch lists due to his close ties with several top cell leaders. His operation had slowed tremendously after getting raided on numerous occasions. Forced to deal in diamonds more honestly, he almost dropped off the radar after several years. But when Bahar reportedly reached out to him to set up a meeting with one of her top lieutenants Kahlid Salib, the U.S. intelligence community took notice. And the Phoenix Foundation found itself as the one tapped to snuff out this potential threat and serve yet another setback to Bahar and Al Fatihin.

"Any sign of them from your side?" Hawk asked.

"Negative," Black said. "Just dust and sand."

"You'd think they'd pick a more luxurious site, like, say Dubai."

"You can work on your tan out here just as well as you can there," Black said with a chuckle.

"Not when I'm draped underneath all this netting."

"You could've always been an accountant or an insurance salesman if you wanted the life of comfort."

"And boredom."

Black laughed softly. "And you think wallowing in the sand on a warm African day is more exciting?"

Hawk didn't say anything.

"Those accountants and insurance salesmen have it just as boring today but far more comfortable," Black continued. "And I bet they're taking vacations to Dubai whenever the hell they want to instead of having to wait for some terrorist to schedule a clandestine meeting there."

"I just want to shoot something," Hawk said.

"That makes two of us, though I'd prefer the target to something of value."

"Okay, okay, that's enough," Alex said, interrupting the two agents' banter. "Time to stop pining away for better vacations and sounding like the rest of America. You've got company headed your way from the north and south."

Positioned on the west side of the ridge, Hawk slowly turned to his left to see a trail of dust flying behind a black SUV. To his right, he saw a near-identical vehicle storming toward the valley below. While Hawk hadn't enjoyed lying in wait, at least his suffering hadn't been in vain. The intelligence had been perfect, and it was time to ensure that the men and women who obtained the information be rewarded for their sacrifices.

"You want to take out Salib or Jacobs?" Hawk asked.

"Dealer's choice," Black said.

"I'll take Jacobs then. Utilizing children to mine the diamonds is bad enough, but then you launder them to support terrorists. It doesn't get much more lowlife in my book than that."

"Can't argue with that."

A long paused followed before Alex chimed in again. "Before these scumbags are eliminated, Blunt told me that we need a visual verification of their identities as well as audio of the conversation."

"What on Earth for?" Hawk asked.

"I don't know," she said. "Something to do with proving to the Sudanese government that we weren't up to anything nefarious since they gave us permission to be on their soil."

"Like they could discern what's right and wrong," Hawk said. "These people butcher each other to death for being from the wrong side of the street."

"Not to mention they're probably involved somehow in this whole laundering scheme," Black chimed in.

"It's barely noon and you two are teeming with cynicism," Alex said. "What a perfect pair."

"Cynical? That's all you consider us?" Black said. "If that's my worst attribute, I'll take it, especially since that's what usually keeps me alive."

"Never change, Black," Hawk said. "Though I'd say you aren't nearly as cynical as you should sometimes be."

"Maybe I'm just good enough that I haven't been captured as many times as you have, Hawk."

Hawk shrugged off the zinger. "I'm still alive though—and still the worst nightmare for these punks."

Black chuckled. "Time to confirm their identities before we light them up."

The two vehicles had skidded to a stop, kicking up another cloud of dust to join the one already wafting through the valley from their respective trips to the meeting site.

"What are they waiting on?" Black asked.

"I don't know," Hawk said. "But I don't like this."

Hawk studied the scene, which, for the moment, was little more than two SUVs parked directly in front of one another in the middle of the Nuba Mountains. The tinted windows made it difficult to see any movement inside as neither door on his side budged.

"Anything on your side?" Hawk asked.

"Negative," Black said. "They're both glued to their seats from what I can tell. About all I can see is the driver of the SUV on the south—and he hasn't even flinched. His hands are still gripping the steering wheel as if he's about to take off again."

"There's no way they could've spotted us," Hawk said.

"Those assumptions are what get you in trouble," Alex said.

"I set up a motion detector perimeter for a mile around us," Black said. "I haven't heard the first notification that even an animal penetrated the line. How the hell could they know where we are?"

"Call it a hunch," Alex said. "Evana Bahar learned from one of the best. It took us years to catch Karif Fazil."

"He was the epitome of caution," Hawk said. "And it's exactly why one of his subordinates requested a meeting in a place like this."

"But he still made a mistake," Black said.

"His only mistake was his pride," Hawk said. "Otherwise, we'd still be trying to squelch him as opposed to simply snuffing out Al Fatihin before it builds any significant momentum."

After a few seconds, Hawk noticed a glint of sunshine off the window as it was slowly slung open.

"Hold tight, everyone," Hawk said. "It looks like we've got movement."

"Roger that," Black said. "Got something

happening here on this side with the south SUV."

"Just a reminder that we need visual confirmation before laying waste to these guys," Alex said. "Does everyone copy?"

"Copy that," Black and Hawk both said in unison.

Hawk took out a small recording device and pointed it in the valley below at the two men who were walking toward one another to shake hands.

"Are you getting all this, Alex?" he asked.

"Your signal is coming in strong," she said. "I'm running their faces through the database right now just to make sure."

"And their voices?" Hawk asked.

"I can barely make out what they're saying," she said. "Can you tweak the audio?"

"Negative," Hawk said. "You'll have to boost it on your end."

"If you've got something on the audio, the video should suffice," Black said. "I say it's time to take a shot."

Alex let out a string of expletives, reverberating in Hawk's ears.

"What's that all about?" Hawk asked.

"You guys have company," Alex said. "I missed it while I was trying to secure all these requirements."

A helicopter popped over one of the mountains behind Hawk and zoomed past him, heading straight for the ravine where the two SUVs were parked.

"Black, you got a shot?" Hawk asked.

"I had one, but it's gone. They both just got into one of the vehicles."

"I saw that, but it wasn't on my side."

"It's too late now," Black said. "We're going to have to wait until they get out again. Or we could just light up these vehicles."

"No explosions," Alex said. "That was part of the agreement. We cannot attract attention out here."

"I don't need to blow anything up to kill everybody inside," Black said.

"Resist the urge," Alex said. "One of the drivers is a Sudanese national. If we kill him, we're going to be brought in on charges of murder."

"Hang on a second," Hawk said. "The back passenger side door on the car from the north is opening."

"I see it," Alex said. "If you can take the shot—"

Hawk had already tuned her out and was focusing on lining up his shot. He was almost sure that he had Jacobs sighted in before disaster struck.

The chopper descended just to the west of the vehicles, kicking up the equivalent of a sandstorm. As a result, Hawk lost visual with Jacobs and Salib.

"They're gone," Hawk said. "I can't even tell what vehicle they're in now."

"If they're even in one of those SUVs," Alex said.

"You got a shot, Black?" Hawk asked.

There was no reply.

"Black, you read me? You have a shot?"

Still nothing.

"Damn it, Black. Answer me," Hawk said.

"They're not getting away," Black said, sounding as if he were out of breath.

"You're not down there, are you?" Hawk asked.

"Affirmative," Black said.

"You're not thinking straight," Hawk said. "I can't give you any cover from up here with the way that chopper is stirring up all that sand."

"I won't need it," Black said.

Hawk watched as his colleague scrambled down to the valley floor. Then he vanished in the midst of the swirling dust.

"You have a visual on him from the satellite feed?" Hawk asked.

"No," Alex said. "I can't see anything. The heat signatures aren't even working very well in the desert."

"I'm going after him," Hawk said.

"Don't you dare," Alex said. "You stay put. We can't have both of you captured or shot. Blunt is gonna lose it when he hears about this."

"I don't care," Hawk said. "I've already lost too much recently, and I'm not about to lose a team member without a fight."

Hawk slithered out from beneath his blind and leaped over a boulder. Hustling down the mountainside, he stayed close to the ground, crouched over with his weapon drawn and trained in the direction of the action. But before he reached the bottom, both SUVs spun around and tore off in the opposite direction from which they came while the helicopter ascended and then rolled away.

Hawk sank to his knees in the sand and glared skyward.

"He's gone, isn't he?" Alex asked.

Hawk didn't answer. He couldn't bring himself to utter a response aloud.

Black was gone—and Hawk didn't have a clue who had taken his partner.

CHAPTER 2

Washington, D.C.

HAWK SLUMPED INTO A CHAIR at the conference table in the Phoenix Foundation's offices. He grimaced as he rubbed his face with both hands and sighed. A week had passed since Titus Black vanished into thin air amidst a mission that ended in almost the worst way possible. While the loop was kept tight on the assignment, Hawk couldn't help but think someone leaked the details about their operation to Al Fatihin or Freddie Jacobs. Either way, Hawk had lost a fellow soldier who was every bit an equal in the field.

J.D. Blunt lumbered into the office and swatted Hawk with a manila folder.

"Get your head out of your ass, Hawk," Blunt said. "So what? Things went sideways in Sudan. We'll figure out a way to get our man back."

Hawk shook his head and leaned forward, resting

21

on his arms. "I can't put my finger on it, but this felt like a setup somehow. I'd almost bet on the fact that we were played."

"Then why are you still here?" Blunt asked.

"Maybe they didn't think we would send a pair of operatives," Alex said as she breezed into the room. "Most of Hawk's recent missions have been solo. And if this was a setup, it's clear they wanted Hawk there."

"But I wasn't the one who ran down the hillside," Hawk said.

"You weren't the one who ran down it first," Alex said. "There was a time—"

"I know," Hawk said. "Maybe I'm getting wiser in my old age."

Blunt chuckled. "Let's not go that far. But at least we still have one of you." There was an awkward pause as Blunt studied his two agents. Alex eyed Hawk closely and reached out to him, taking his hand in hers.

"I have a feeling that's not the only thing bothering you, Hawk," Blunt said. "Wanna talk about it?"

"What is this? An intervention?" Hawk asked.

"Hardly," Blunt said. "But I can tell you've been somewhat distant ever since your mother—"

"Don't say it," Hawk said, holding his hands up in a gesture for Blunt to stop. "I don't want to hear the words uttered."

"Ignoring the pain won't make it go away," Alex said.

Hawk nodded. "But you know what will ease it? Catching the son of a bitch who—"

He stopped and sighed before leaning back in his chair again.

"Just give it some time," Blunt said. "The Dallas PD is working on it. I've got some friends in the homicide department, and I know that investigation is still active."

Hawk cast a sideways glance at Blunt. "Are you sure about that?"

"Sure as I am sitting here. I just spoke with Detective Pickens this morning. He said they're still chipping away at it, but it's been rough due to the lack of evidence. They'll find something eventually."

Hawk closed his eyes and shook his head subtly. "I think the worst thing is I never got to have closure. I never saw her body or watched her casket lowered into the ground."

"I know," Blunt said. "But we thought someone was trying to lure you out into the open at the time. You have to understand we made that decision because we thought it was the most prudent."

"I get it," Hawk said. "That doesn't make it any easier though."

"Your paths will cross one day," Blunt said. "And

when they do, I'm sure you'll be ready to bring the killer to justice. In the meantime, we have to stay vigilant and courageous as we battle on against these forces wreaking havoc on our country."

Alex gave Hawk's hand a squeeze before she scooted back in her seat. Hawk forced a smile as he looked at her. Then he mouthed a "thank you" to her before she smiled back.

"My mother used to talk about courage all the time," Hawk said. "She told me that without courage, I'm just an average person trying to survive in life. But she used to tell me all the time, 'Brady, be brave. Be extraordinary.' She was the first person to believe in me like that—and now she's gone. I can hardly stomach the thought, knowing that I'm somehow to blame for all of this. She didn't ask to be hunted down and gutted by some coward just to try to get at me. She was a good woman."

"A great woman," Blunt said.

Hawk nodded. "Well, the best way for me to honor her legacy is to keep doing what she urged me to do, which was to follow my passion for helping others."

"That's something you're damn good at," Blunt said.

He stopped and turned his attention to the television on the back wall. Snatching the remote from the center of the table, Blunt turned the volume up as a reporter shared the details about the government's new focus on centralizing intelligence to better protect the American people.

"Many here on Capitol Hill are calling next week's dedication of the National Security Complex near Langley, Virginia to be one of the most well-attended events of the year from parties on both sides of the aisle," reported Lindsay Baker. "This bipartisan effort serves as a reminder of the power of Congress when representatives put aside their party ideology and do what's best for the country. State officials from all branches will be on hand for the ceremony that marks the dawn of a new era in the way the United States intelligence community gathers information. The NSC will be the hub for every intelligence agency under the auspices of the U.S. government, both civilian and military."

Blunt shook his head and chuckled. "The dawn of a new era? Just cram everyone into one building, and suddenly the public will think your country is safer."

"We weren't invited to join them in their shiny new building, were we?" Alex asked.

"We don't exist, remember?" Blunt said with a wink. "The Phoenix Foundation officially helps with policy, not actual intelligence gathering and logistical security."

Linda, Blunt's secretary, rapped on the outside of the door. "Pardon the interruption, sir, but you have a call on line one from CIA Deputy Director Al White. He said he needs to speak with you and it's urgent."

Hawk bolted upright in his chair. "White wants to speak with you? I thought Fortner had a closed loop on who knew about us."

"Apparently, the loop has expanded," Blunt said before turning to his secretary. "Thanks, Linda. I'll take the call in here."

Blunt waited until Linda shut the door before he answered the phone. "It's been a long time, Al."

"The last time I saw you was at your supposed funeral," White said with his thick South Carolina drawl. "But only one of us showed up."

"Sorry for all the trouble and pain," Blunt said. "It was, unfortunately, necessary for me to disappear."

White laughed. "Don't worry, J.D. I didn't shed any tears. I was just wondering if you were going to bequeath me that signed Nolan Ryan baseball in your office."

"I've got something better. How about we go hunting with him the next time you're in Texas."

"I like the sound of that."

"Well, Al, I wanted to let you know that you're on speaker with a couple of members of my team here—and I'm sure you didn't call to just catch up."

"Certainly not, though I did just learn about your organization about a week ago in a meeting."

Blunt scowled. "Only Fortner and one other special agent were supposed to know what we're up to here at the Phoenix Foundation. Who told you?"

"Fortner let it slip in a meeting with several other department heads last week."

"That's unusual," Blunt said. "He's careful to avoid disclosing any intel like that."

"Well, we were discussing our options in handling an issue down in South America with a drug lord who has moved into the illegal arms sales business. This particular guy happened to be the brother of the country's president and we couldn't handle things how we normally do. So he suggested an alternative method, which was your foundation."

"Wonderful," Blunt said. "The last thing we need is for everyone figuring out the true nature of what we do here."

"I wouldn't worry about it," White said. "It was only Casper, Riggins, and Mitchell in the meeting."

"I always worry about Henry Riggins," Blunt said. "He was a thorn in my side when I served in the Senate."

"Riggins is harmless."

Blunt knit his brow and tapped his pen on the

table. "So, did you just call me to tell me that the cat's out of the bag? Or is there something else you wanted to discuss?"

"No, there is a reason for my call. I wanted to let you know that we received a curious communiqué last night from the Middle East that I thought you might be interested in."

"One of my good friends over there wanting my address so he could send me a Christmas card?" Blunt said with a chuckle.

"This one had to do with a proposed prisoner exchange from a source we verified that works with Al Fatihin. Can you list your roster of agents for me?"

"Come on, Al. You know that's classified. Only Fortner, a special agent, and the president know who's working here in the special projects division. That loop needs to remain tighter."

"I just thought you would want to know because if the prisoner is one of your agents, I'd hate for him to get stranded over there."

Blunt chuckled. "And you think I can just whip up some extraction team out of thin air to rescue him."

"No, I just thought we might be able to make an exchange."

"And negotiate with terrorists? Fortner's not gonna go for that."

White sighed. "Look, I'm trying to help you out here. Are you even missing an agent?"

"What's the name?"

"So you are missing an agent?"

"The name, Al."

"Well, it's classified, J.D., and—"

"Are we gonna do some bureaucratic dance now after even protocol has been broken?"

"Fine. The name they gave me was Titus Black."

Hawk's eyes widened as he glanced back and forth between Blunt and Alex. A smile spread across Alex's lips as she mouthed the words "he's alive" to Hawk.

There was a long pause as the trio exchanged knowing glances.

"J.D., are you still there?" White asked.

"Let me get back to you," Blunt said. "And, Al?"

"What?"

"Thanks. I trust you'll remain discreet about the fact that you disclosed this information to us."

"Always."

Blunt ended the call and rubbed his hands together. "Sounds like we need to get to work."

CHAPTER 3

THE NEXT DAY at the Phoenix Foundation offices, Hawk and Alex prepared for the prisoner exchange by plotting out all of the details necessary for a smooth operation. Blunt worked through back channels to arrange for the return of a high profile asset, noting how difficult it was without being able to give out Black's name. By the end of the afternoon, they all reconvened to discuss their progress and share their prospects for a successful swap.

Hawk wore a hint of a smile on his lips as he settled into his seat next to Alex.

"What is it?" Blunt asked before snipping off the end of his cigar and gnawing on it. "You don't look nearly as depressed as you did yesterday."

"I'm not sure losing Ramin Torabi is that big of a blow for us," Hawk said. "I did a little digging, and I think I know why Evana prioritized his return."

"And are you going to tell us why, or do you want to make us guess?" Blunt asked.

"Ramin is family, second cousins with Evana to be precise," Hawk said. "It's not like he's some key cog in the newly-formed Al Fatihin wheel."

"And if he were, it'd be a surefire way to tip their hand," Alex said. "Good observation."

Blunt shrugged. "Maybe you're right. However, I feel like there's something more to this that we're not seeing. This has all the makings of another setup."

"I wouldn't be so sure," Hawk said. "I think this was clearly a ploy to secure the return of Ramin, which is significant for reasons other than the mere construction of a viable terrorist group."

"Pray tell, what is that reason?" Blunt asked before shielding his mouth with the back of his hand and turning toward Alex. "Remind me never to give Hawk analyst access again. He's a little too eager to show off in this meeting."

Alex laughed softly before cutting her eyes toward Hawk.

"Will you two knock it off," Hawk said. "This is beyond serious."

"Okay, fine," Blunt said. "Please continue. Just don't make me guess anymore about what you found, all right?"

Hawk nodded and proceeded to share his findings. "Ramin also happens to be the son of Amir Torabi, the HadithTel cell phone magnate. He's worth nearly a billion dollars, and HadithTel is experiencing significant growth throughout the region. It's the perfect way for her to dip into his deep pockets and get some under-the-table funding."

"Ramin has proven worthless when it comes to gleaning information, so if we trade him away, we're not losing anything," Blunt said. "But the relationship between HadithTel and Al Fatihin will be an important one for CIA analysts to delve into."

"So, you think trading him won't be a problem?" Hawk asked.

Blunt shrugged. "Depends on if they have some other value for him that we don't know about it."

"I can't imagine what that would be," Hawk said.

"That's because you're a field agent," Blunt said with a wink.

"Are you suggesting that I didn't do a good job with this?"

Blunt waved his hand dismissively. "Not at all, despite your eagerness to impress. However, sometimes there are other elements in play that we aren't necessarily privy too. Even with the supposed cooperation between all the agencies, we can't always access everything we need."

"So, what's next?" Hawk asked.

"I'll make a phone call and see what I can get done."

"Who are you going to call?" Alex asked. "Fortner?"

Blunt shook his head. "I'm calling the president."

* * *

BLUNT EASED INTO HIS CHAIR before dialing President Young's secretary. She said that the president was in a meeting and he would call back as soon as he was finished.

With the few extra minutes to prepare, Blunt mulled over the best approach to address Young. He wasn't likely to be warm to the idea of trading prisoners with a terrorist cell, but if he could be convinced, maybe Fortner wouldn't put up such a fuss about it.

A few minutes later, Young called back and the conversation started out just as Blunt had imagined it would after explaining the details of the situation.

"Come on, J.D.," Young said. "You know our long-standing policy is that we don't negotiate with terrorists."

"You know that's a bunch of bullshit," Blunt said. "We've made all kinds of concessions with various terrorist groups over the years. It's why she even asked in the first place. We trot out that mantra for the press every time there's a hostage situation, but it's not being taken seriously or even respected. These scumbags know the truth about how we operate.

Besides, it's not like this is some public demand."

"Who else knows about this?"

"Just a handful of people within the CIA—and now you."

Young sighed. "I trust Fortner. It's why I moved him out of the Pentagon and put him in charge of the agency. If he's not on board with this, neither am I."

"You know you can influence him to do this, even if he's stubborn."

"This agent must be very important to you. I'd expect you to act this way about Hawk, but I didn't realize you were so fond of Black."

"We need him," Blunt said. "He's proven his worth many times over, especially in the way he's been able to penetrate Obsidian's inner circle. If we're going to take them down, it's imperative that we get him back."

"I'm sure you have other agents who are more than capable of that task."

"I only have two field agents at the moment, and I'm not out there actively recruiting. I only deploy the most elite operatives into the field. And right now, that's just Hawk and Black."

"I'm sorry, J.D. I just can't do it. We haven't done this under my presidency, and I feel like it would set a dangerous precedent."

"The precedent has already been set. You'd be bucking the trend by refusing."

"Okay, I've heard your argument, but the answer is still no. Find another way to get him back."

Blunt fumed inside but restrained himself. "Thank you for your time, Mr. President."

The line went dead.

Blunt pounded his fist on his desk and let out a string of expletives as he got up and paced around his office. He thought for sure Young would be an ally. After cooling off, Blunt visited Hawk and Alex, who were studying their computer screens.

"I just got off the phone with the president," Blunt said as he entered the room and shut the door behind him.

Hawk and Alex both stopped what they were doing and spun around in their chairs to face Blunt.

"And?" Hawk said.

"And he shot down the exchange," Blunt said.

"You still haven't asked Fortner, have you?" Alex asked.

"I know Fortner, and he has a hard and fast rule about negotiating with terrorists. His policy is that agents shouldn't get caught in the first place. And they know the consequences if they do."

"You're sure he won't budge, even if the request comes from you?" Alex asked.

Blunt shook his head. "Fortner would do just about anything to help me and my agents, but this is a line I know he won't cross."

"So what are our options now?" Hawk asked. "We can't just forget about Black and move on. We know he's alive. You have to press this further. Besides, I've been thinking about this whole situation, and I have an idea of how we can leverage this exchange to an even greater advantage for us."

Blunt settled into a chair next to Hawk's desk. "I'm listening."

"Well, do you remember the agent who vanished from the U.N. who's still on the lam?"

Blunt nodded. "Go on."

"The only picture we had of him was with Evana Bahar," Hawk said. "So, what if we agreed to the exchange but told her that the terms were she had to be there?"

"She'd never go for that," Blunt said.

"Maybe, but it's a negotiation. We say without her there, no deal."

Alex shook her head. "You'd be risking Black's life on a hunch that she'd agree to be there. You can't do that."

"I don't think it'd be much of a risk, to be honest," Hawk said. "She wants Ramin back so she can fund future operations. Acquiring him from the U.S. would earn her an immense amount of favor with Ramin's father, resulting in a huge windfall of cash.

Without that, she's going to be living hand to mouth, which isn't exactly the best way to become relevant as a terrorist organization."

"And what if she refuses to cooperate with you when you get there?" Blunt asked.

"I will be very persuasive," Hawk said.

Blunt pulled the cigar out of his mouth. "That's not what I asked."

"I have a plan for how to handle that situation. She'll talk. Trust me."

Blunt nodded. "Okay, I'll make a call, but you better be right."

"I don't know about all this," Alex said. "Tying Black's fate to a decision like this seems rather frivolous as if we're playing with his life."

"It was Black's frivolous decision to run down the mountain that put us in this situation," Blunt said. "I'm sure he's had plenty of time to think about the repercussions."

Alex sighed. "Fine. I just want the record to show that I'm not a fan of this move."

"Duly noted," Blunt said. "Now, if you two will excuse me, I need to have a chat with our good friend Al White."

Blunt trudged back to his office and closed his door. He returned to his chair and dialed White's number.

"We talked it through," Blunt began. "And we see

a big opportunity here to not only secure one of our best agents but also to make some headway in another operation we're working on."

"Okay," White said. "Their exchange offer was presented to us as a quick swap."

"And I want you to go back with a counteroffer. I want you to tell them that Evana Bahar has to be the one to make the exchange."

"I doubt she's going to be interested in having some protracted conversation with one of your agents while there are snipers all around."

"We can set up parameters to put everyone at ease," Hawk said. "The bottom line is that we'd be fools to pass up an opportunity to question her. If she can help us—"

"What makes you so sure she'd be willing to talk if she even decides to show up?"

"I have a very persuasive agent."

White chuckled.

"That's the same reaction I had," Blunt said. "But I've learned to stop questioning my agents when they're willing to risk everything to get what we need."

White sighed. "I'll make contact with Al Fatihin and see if Evana Bahar will agree to these terms. But I wouldn't hold my breath if I were you."

Blunt hung up and leaned back in his chair. All he could do now was wait for a response.

CHAPTER 4

Undisclosed location, Afghanistan

EVANA BAHAR STROKED HER silky smooth locks while staring at the message transmitted to her by the CIA contact. She tried to suppress a smile that had crept across her lips. As she closed her eyes, she imagined what her life would look like with Amir Torabi helping her secure funding for Al Fatihin. No more clandestine meetings with sketchy bankers. No more wondering if she was being set up every time she tried to come to terms with an underworld money launderer. Instead of wasting time worrying about money, she could be plotting about how to weaken America and bring the imperialistic nation to its knees.

She snapped out of her daydream when Kahlid Salib strode into her makeshift office in the adobe house she'd chosen as the organization's headquarters for the week.

"You wanted to see me?" Salib asked.

"Yes, I wanted to thank you again for your work in Sudan," she said. "The Americans took the bait before, and they're taking it again."

"That's outstanding news."

"However, there is a catch."

Salib's eyebrows shot upward. "A catch?"

"They want me to be at the exchange personally."

Salib scowled and shook his head. "Absolutely not. That kind of demand is out of the question. They'd never send the president to a prisoner exchange if you made that as a stipulation. It's just ridiculous."

"I am intrigued by what they want."

"They want to bring you to justice for the charges they've already levied against you through their American media mouthpieces," Salib said. "They've already branded you as a butcher, all while completely unaware of how their own government routinely murders hundreds of—"

"Enough," Evana said as she raised her hand. "I don't need you to explain the hypocritical nature of the American military machine. I simply want to stop it. And that's why I'm seriously considering taking them up on this offer."

"If given the opportunity, they will kill you."

She shrugged. "And if they do, I know that Al Fatihin will be in your competent hands."

"You swore to Karif that you would carry out his legacy and see this to the end. If you're dead, that will be a difficult promise to keep."

"You worry too much," Evana said as she stood up from behind her desk and sauntered over to Salib. She gently put her hands on his chest before slipping her hands behind his back and interlocking her fingers.

His steely gaze met hers. "This hardly feels like the time for a romantic gesture."

"What are you so afraid of?" she asked. "Do you think you're going to lose me?"

Salib laughed nervously and looked aside.

"I know how you feel about me," she said. "There's no reason for you to hide it any longer."

"I'm a warrior, and we have an important mission. We can't be distracted by passions of the flesh."

Evana released him and eased back a step before ripping his shirt open. Then she drew close again, caressing his rock hard muscles on his bare chest.

Salib took a deep breath before looking down at Evana. He moved in for a kiss. Almost instantly, she shoved him and backed away.

"What are you doing?" she asked.

Salib's face turned a rosy hue. "I thought that you—"

"That was a test and you failed," Evana said.

"You are worried about a little meeting with the Americans that could change the fortunes of this organization, but I believe I'm the one who needs to be worried. Apparently, all it takes is a little attention from a woman along with some simple flattery and you'll crumble."

"I'm sorry," Salib said. "I didn't mean anything by it. It's just that—"

"Save your explanations. I'm not interested in hearing your justification for embracing my advances, especially when you have a wife and children at home. What kind of Muslim man are you? Certainly not the kind who takes his vows seriously."

Salib hung his head for a moment before looking up. "Again, I apologize. That's not the kind of man that I am, but I must take responsibility for my actions. However, I still feel compelled to urge you to change your mind about agreeing to the Americans' terms regarding the exchange."

She smiled and returned to her chair behind her desk. "There aren't many agents I thought they would even be willing to consider an exchange for. But I believe we struck the perfect balance between an operative the CIA cares deeply about and a prisoner they see little value in. To them, Ramin is simply occupying space in a cell. They know by now that he's never going to provide them with actionable intelligence. It's an easy decision, even for a government who likes to thump its chest and brag about how they never negotiate with terrorists."

"In that case, I will defer to your judgment and pray to Allah that you are not walking into a trap."

"I don't trust them, but I don't believe they will try any tricks when it comes to Agent Black," she said. "It's me they need to worry about. I have my own special plans for the Americans."

* * *

BLUNT POURED A GLASS of bourbon and stared at the photo of the mystery man from the U.N.

"Who are you?" Blunt asked aloud.

He peered closer at the man's face before placing a loupe over the picture and squinting. After several seconds, Blunt sighed and then leaned back in his chair. There weren't any identifying marks—jewelry, clothes, briefcase, or watch—that gave Blunt any clues.

He would've preferred to figure out who the other man was by some other means. His worst nightmare was allowing Hawk to walk into a trap and Al Fatihin taking out his two best agents in one fell swoop. But desperation had pushed him to this point, though he was sure Evana Bahar would never agree to the terms of their exchange.

Blunt was in the middle of a long pull on his drink when the phone rang. He wiped the corners of his mouth with his index finger and thumb before answering the call.

"This is Blunt," he said.

"J.D., Al White here. I've got an answer for you."

"So soon? Must be a no."

"That's what I thought too, but she agreed to your parameters. Morocco. Three days. I'll send over all the other details about the meeting tomorrow. Just thought I'd let you know the good news as soon as possible so you can begin prepping for the exchange."

"Excellent, Al."

Blunt hung up and glanced back at the photo.

"We're going to find out who you are soon enough," Blunt said. "I just hope it's not too late."

CHAPTER 5

Three Days Later
Morocco

HAWK RAISED HIS ARMS to be checked for any weapons by the Al Fatihin guard. After a thorough frisking, Hawk was cleared and ushered into an empty room with Ramin Torabi. The two had only been together a few hours, united at the airport after Ramin took a CIA transport plane ride across the Atlantic and Hawk arrived on the Phoenix Foundation's private jet.

Ramin's hands were zip-tied in front of him, further diminishing his stature. With wire-rimmed glasses and a thin physique, Ramin appeared unimposing. Hawk studied the man, wondering how he fell into fighting with Al Hasib.

"Are you looking forward to seeing your father again?" Hawk asked.

Ramin gave Hawk a sideways glance before looking away with a sneer.

"I never really knew my father," Hawk said, continuing his effort to engage Ramin in conversation. "If he's still alive and willing to be in your life—"

"You know nothing about my life," Ramin snapped.

"Your father obviously wants you back."

"He wants me back so he can parade me into public and brag about his son. Over the years, he made it clear to me that he doesn't care what I want."

Hawk nodded knowingly. "So, that's what attending Stanford was all about? Fulfilling his dreams for you?"

"I hated being on that campus every day. All I heard were students complaining about how their parents wouldn't let them fly first class on spring break vacations to Bali or how the sports car their father bought them was previously owned for a year. Meanwhile, people all across our region are barely surviving due to the unjust occupation by the Americans."

"Stanford doesn't look like the rest of America, that much I know. There are people who are struggling to survive there too."

Ramin shrugged. "At least they don't live in fear of dying from an explosion while walking to the market."

"Based on how you loathe such things, I find it odd that you joined Al Hasib, the same group responsible for bombing plenty of markets."

"We always go after the Americans and their war machine. Sometimes there is collateral damage."

"That statement sounded just like ones I've heard from American generals. You don't have any moral high ground to stand on."

"I have the Quran, and it's very detailed about how to handle infidels."

Hawk scowled and shook his head. "You need to find true salam in your life."

"I'm sure you would feel differently if you watched an American soldier slit the throat of your best friend in front of you."

Hawk shifted restlessly in his chair. The conversation had grown uncomfortable, especially as he reflected on all the anger he harbored for his mother's killer.

Moments later, the door swung open and Black entered the room, accompanied by Evana Bahar. She seemed different this time, almost eerily calm. Sliding into the chair across from him, she sat down and clasped her hands together in front of her on the table.

"Mr. Hawk," she began, "I suspected you might be behind this, but I'm surprised to see you sitting here. You're taking quite the risk in being the one to negotiate this exchange."

"I didn't take you for the assured mutual destruction type," Hawk said. "I simply wanted to ask you a few questions."

She eyed the manila folder lying in front of him. "What's in there?"

Hawk placed his hand on top of it and shook his head. "After we've made the exchange."

She nodded, and they both got up and ushered their respective prisoners across the room before leading them outside to stand with their armed guards. When Hawk and Evana returned, they took their previous seats and resumed their discussion.

"I was intrigued by your terms," she said. "I couldn't help but wonder what you wanted from me. And you, of all people, weren't exactly cordial to me the last time we met."

"You had a missile and were trying to kill the president. That will always make me a little hostile."

"Very well then," she said. "Let's get on with it. What did you want to ask me?"

Hawk opened the folder and slid several pictures across the table. "I was wondering if you could help me identify the man in these pictures."

She craned her neck and glanced at the images before leaning back and furrowing her brow. "Did you honestly think I would just blurt out the man's name to you?" she said with a soft laugh. "You're more naïve than I ever took you to be."

"I'd be disappointed if you did," Hawk said. "But there's more to this story. For all our differing ideologies, we must put them aside for a moment."

"You think it's as simple as our having a different ideology? There is a right and a wrong here—and I'm on the right side, no matter how brainwashed your country has made you."

Hawk sighed. "If you don't help me, you may not have anything to fight for."

"Why? Is this man going to destroy the world?" she said while rolling her eyes. "You must know that you're wasting both our time." Evana stood up, pushing her chair back with her knees.

"Please, sit down," Hawk said. "I'm not finished. There's something you need to know about him. Have you ever heard of an organization called Obsidian?"

She shrugged. "I've heard the name, but it's a legend. There's no such group. It's just a name thrown out to scare people from time to time."

"No, it's very real as my good friend Titus Black can attest to. And if Obsidian has their way, they're going to control the entire world one way or another. Just last month, they intended to unleash a plague on the world that would've been devastating and killed millions, if not billions. But we stopped them. However, the man in that photo with you escaped, and we need to find him."

She shook her head. "I'm sorry, Mr. Hawk. Your effort is to be commended, but I'm not going to reveal his name."

* * *

EVANA SWALLOWED HARD as she glanced down at the pictures in front of her. Her mouth was dry and she wanted some water, though there wasn't any in the room. She felt the sweat beading up on her forehead as the American agent refused to yield in his quest to discover whom the man was depicted next to her. She was shocked to see images of herself seated at a table with him, laughing and smiling.

Could he really be working with Obsidian?

The prying eyes hadn't captured her most recent conversation with him, which took place only four months ago. However, she remembered the meeting, though she was unaware that there was a security camera in the room. Her advance team claimed to have cleared the French bakery as a safe place to meet, devoid of any prying eyes. Apparently, that wasn't the case. She made a note to find out who was serving on her detail that morning.

While she acted as if Obsidian was an urban myth, she knew it was real. But the extent to which she viewed it as a threat? She had dismissed it years ago. And she still hadn't considered the organization as being capable of doing anything to disrupt the world on any significant level. But there was no way her friend would work with them. He was too dedicated to real causes, not the kind that would simply seek power for power's sake. She hadn't thought about that meeting until confronted by the pictures in front of her.

"He's been in the wind for about six months now," the American said. "We need to find him before it's too late."

"What exactly did he do?"

He shrugged. "We're not sure. We just know he was working with some high-level operatives with Obsidian and may be part of a far more sinister plan, one greater than you or I could dream up, much less execute."

She winced in pain as she studied the images again, not from the discomfort of being pressed for answers but from her churning stomach. Clutching her midsection, she doubled over and took a deep breath.

"Are you all right, Evana?" the American asked.

"I'm fine," she said as she eased herself upright again. "Everything is perfectly fine."

"How long have you been pregnant?" he asked.

Her face flushed red and she looked away, turning her gaze toward the floor.

"It's true, isn't it?" he said.

"You don't know what you're talking about," she said. "I haven't been feeling well lately. It's just a stomach cramp."

"If Obsidian unleashes that plague, you might survive, but your baby won't. Infants, small children, and elderly adults are the most likely to die. Protecting your son or daughter requires that you do what you can to stop Obsidian. Otherwise, we'll all be dead, and what will it matter then?"

The American's argument made sound, logical sense, but it didn't persuade her. How could it? What gave her the right to disclose the photographed man's location after all he had done for her? She concluded nothing did and dug her heels in against the begging.

"I'm not pregnant—though I'm not one to live my life in fear of all the hypothetical scenarios. And as proof, I'm right here in front of a man who tried to throw me out of a helicopter."

"It wasn't personal," he said.

"Pardon me for taking it as such. Since it seems we've reached an impasse, I'll be on my way now. See you soon, Mr. Hawk."

"I'll be looking forward to it," he said.

She exited the room and was scuttled away by her guard, who kept his gun drawn and trained behind him until they rounded the corner. When they reached a place of safety, she turned toward Ramin and gave him a hug.

"It's so good to see you, Ramin," she said.

"Thank you for saving me," he said. "But please don't take me to my father. I will serve Al Fatihin as long as I never have to spend another minute in his presence."

She shook her head and clucked her tongue. "Oh, Ramin. You've been held captive for far too long by those animals. You might be interested to know that your father has changed—and all for the better."

CHAPTER 6

Washington, D.C.

HAWK AND BLACK GATHERED quietly around the conference table and waited for Blunt to saunter into the room. Two days had passed since the failed attempt to extract the identity of the man in the photograph from Evana Bahar, even though it was always a long shot. Hawk bit his lip and shook his head as he pondered how to handle another operational failure. Losing was getting old fast.

Blunt hobbled into the room with a stack of folders tucked beneath his arms. He was working over another cigar in his mouth when he dropped everything down on the spot in front of his chair and fell into it with a sigh.

"I think I need to hire some more analysts," he said. "Or at least find some agents who aren't so reckless."

Black looked down at the floor before making

eye contact with Blunt. "I'm sorry, sir. I know that I've caused you quite a bit of grief over the affair in Sudan. I thought I had an opening, so I went for it. Unfortunately, things didn't pan out."

"You just spent nearly two weeks as a prisoner of Al Fatihin after getting set up—and you just shrug it off and say things didn't pan out? It was an unmitigated disaster, that's what it was. And we had to give up a terrorist just to keep your head attached to your shoulders."

"And I'm most grateful for that, sir," Black said. "In hindsight, I can see how it appeared to be a foolish course of action. But in the moment, I only wanted to make the mission a success."

"Well, you failed," Blunt said. "And not only did you fail, we failed the American people by releasing a terrorist who's now far more motivated to strike back at us after behind held captive. He may have been worthless before for his operational knowledge, but he's certain to be a menace after being reunited with Al Fatihin."

"Again, I'm sorry, sir," Black said. "I wish there was something I could do to reverse what's already happened."

Blunt ignored Black and turned his steely gaze toward Hawk.

"And then there's you," Blunt said. "You thought

Evana Bahar would just volunteer the information about our mystery man. Need I remind you, she's not running a faux charity anymore. She's the freaking leader of a terrorist cell that's hell-bent on wreaking havoc on U.S. interests."

"I understand, sir. Convincing her to help us was a long shot, though I did glean some intel from our meeting."

"What? That's she's pregnant? Big deal," Blunt said, waving his hand dismissively. "We need the kind of information that will lead to the capture of this man if we're ever going to find out what really happened at the U.N. that night or figure out what Obsidian is planning next."

Alex stormed into the room and flung a folder onto the table. "Gentlemen, I just solved our little problem. I know who our mystery man is."

Hawk stared up at his wife, mouth agape. "You figured it out? How in the world did—"

She sat down next to him while the men sifted through the photos spilling out on the table.

"In this day and age, it's almost impossible to be this off the grid," she said. "With CCTV cameras everywhere gathering images and collecting them in a centralized database that we share worldwide with other agencies, the chances of someone being this mysterious and never appearing in any stills or videos while moving between countries made me wonder if there was some other way he could've subverted the system."

"And what did you find?" Blunt asked.

"Well, I put this project on the backburner a few days ago, hoping that Hawk would get Evana Bahar to talk. But when that didn't work, I resumed my research and came across a posting in a dark web chat room where one user was bragging about how slight reconstruction surgery was enough to throw off enough of the data points used in facial recognition software. The poster even listed the easiest places to tweak to fool the system."

"That's how you found this guy? On a dark web chat room?" Black asked as he studied one of the photos.

"No, I took his photo and adjusted the suggested points to come up with an old image of the guy and then inserted it back into the system. That's when I came up with this name—Dr. Daniel Becker."

"Are you sure this is the same guy?" Hawk asked as he held up a picture.

Alex nodded before grabbing the folder and sifting to the last image, which showed Becker in an older photo next to her simulation of him.

"See for yourself," she said.

"How do you know that you didn't just tweak the

image of our mystery man just enough and come up with a spitting image of Becker?" Blunt asked.

"I wondered the same thing until I came across this nugget while doing a little background research on the doc," she said. "He used to work as a fundraiser with Evana Bahar when he had a practice in London. What are the chances of her knowing the old Dr. Becker and a guy who looked just like the new one?"

"Slim to none," Hawk said. "This is our guy."

Alex dropped another folder onto the table. "But that isn't all. Guess who else Dr. Becker had ties to?"

"Out with it," Blunt said. "You and Hawk have to stop with these quiz show presentations."

"Katarina Petrov, the same Katarina that ran The Chamber," Alex said.

"What does this guy do exactly?" Black asked.

"I'm still a bit mystified as to his relationship with both of these groups since he's a well-respected doctor, now practicing in Geneva," Alex said. "His CV reads like some super doctor. You wouldn't believe the number of times he's consulted with the World Health Organization. He's also been the lead doctor on several epidemic cases in Africa and the Middle East. From a legal standpoint, he's spotless. But I found some loose links between key people with The Chamber and Al Fatihin. Then he's at the United Nations the day Obsidian attempted to infect the world."

"Too much smoke not to be fire," Blunt said. "I agree with this analysis. Great work, Alex."

"Thank you, sir."

"This is impressive, how you did this," Black said. "Have you ever considered a career in espionage?"

"There are days I wish I hadn't—and then there are days like today," she said as a big smile spread across her face.

"Amazing, honey," Hawk said.

"I also figured out why Evana Bahar wasn't so keen on turning on him," Alex said. "Apparently, Dr. Becker used some experimental treatment to save Evana's eldest daughter, who was diagnosed with a rare form of brain cancer at the age of two."

"When did you find out that she had a daughter?" Hawk asked. "I had no idea she was ever married."

"According to any official government records, she wasn't," Alex said. "But Dr. Becker wrote about working with a woman who ran a charity in London and how he helped cure her daughter. The timeline fits for when she was meeting with him, including several pictures time-stamped before and after the time of this article of the two of them together. And some of them looked rather chummy."

"Are you suggesting what I think you are?" Blunt asked.

"I'm not saying anything definitively on this, but all the signs point to the two of them having some sort of relationship that extended beyond his help in attracting London's wealthiest donors to several fundraisers to help with her refugee relocation charity."

Black chuckled. "This blows away my preconceived idea of what a terrorist is supposed to look like."

"Welcome to the twenty-first century," Alex said, "where you can be a stay-at-home mom and terrorist. The sky's the limit."

"Maybe it's how these Muslim women are getting rid of deadbeat husbands," Black cracked. "Just convince them to blow themselves up in the name of Islam and you don't have to worry about the shame of divorce, which I hear is quite the burden for Muslims."

"Cute," Blunt said. "But that's enough conjecture. Let's just go get Dr. Becker and ask him these questions ourselves."

"Sounds like a great idea to me," Alex said. "Now all we have to do is break into his literal fortress of a home located in the Swiss Alps that used to be a castle."

"And I'm sure you have a plan," Blunt said.

"Of course I do. We're just going to walk through the front door," Alex said before turning to Hawk and Black. "Wheels up in twenty-four hours, gentlemen."

CHAPTER 7

Saint-Cergue, Switzerland

ALEX GRIPPED THE LEATHER steering wheel tightly as she wove up the twisting mountain road. She flashed her lights at a slow car before speeding past it on a short straightaway. Her hair whipped in the wind, nearly destroying the hair-do she had spent over an hour perfecting back at the hotel.

She slowed down and depressed the button recalling the car's roof. Glancing over at Black, she noticed the white knuckles from his hands gripping the car door.

"You all right over there?" she asked.

Black nodded. "You know, when I get into a shootout with a dozen bad guys with semi-automatics guns, I'm not even half afraid as I am right now with you whipping around these corners here."

She chuckled. "Maybe Hawk is justified for insisting on being behind the steering wheel whenever we go somewhere together."

"Maybe I should've been more persistent."

"No, you're just fine," she said. "And you haven't gotten into an accident with me at the helm, have you?"

He shook his head slowly. "We're still not there yet—or back."

"Fine," she said. "You can drive back, but don't complain about how this car handles. It's made for going fast, not for a luxurious ride."

As Alex approached the top of the mountain, less than a mile away from the entrance to the property, she eased off the accelerator and reviewed different elements of the mission with him.

"Do you understand what your role is tonight?" she asked.

He nodded. "Make them think we're indeed a power couple, and do whatever I can to ensure that we get Dr. Becker alone for a while."

"No running around waving your gun," she said.

"And keep your hands to yourself," Hawk said over the coms device.

He was set up nearby in a van to monitor the proceedings via audio and the security camera feed Alex had tapped into before leaving for the gala at Dr. Becker's estate.

Black shook his head. "Don't worry, Hawk. I'll

be the perfect gentlemen, only stealing a kiss if it's absolutely necessary."

Hawk chuckled. "You better be joking."

Alex welcomed the opportunity to dress up in a shimmering silver sequined dress, something she didn't get to do all that often while working for Blunt. Her most common attire consisted of jeans and a sweatshirt. But tonight was different.

Despite such short notice, Alex had secured entrance to the event by calling two Americans— Phillip and Angela Muncie—with invitations and requesting to go in their place. Phillip, who had worked in intelligence for the U.S. government, readily agreed but had to come up with a valid excuse to dissuade his wife from attending. She was passionate about saving the environment and told her husband that she'd been looking forward to the environmental fundraiser for months so she could meet several of her conservation heroes. But in the end, Phillip convinced her to yield her ticket by promising to take her to another event later in the month in Bali.

The event was a who's who in the environmental world with many world leaders there. Because Black looked more like Phillip naturally and that it was possible Hawk had crossed paths with several of the attendees with scurrilous backgrounds, Black earned the nod as the one to escort Alex, posing as the Muncies.

"Are you sure no one is going to recognize you?" Alex asked Black.

He nodded. "I do my best work undercover. Infiltrating impenetrable groups is where Blunt has assigned me for the past several years. And, to be quite frank, I'm not sure I would ever willingly seek out anyone from this group."

"You're not a fan of recycling?" she chided.

"I do my part for the planet. But what really irks me are these elitist snobs who act as if they care about saving the world and implementing harsh sanctions on the regular person while flitting about the globe on their gas-guzzling private jets, unaffected by even the slightest heightened cost for their indulgences. What they don't realize is that we'll probably all end up killing each other before the planet reaches a critical level."

"Don't we both know that all too well," Alex said. "However, I'd ask that you put aside your disdain for these people and be polite and smile and make friendly banter. Can you do that for me?"

Black sighed. "I promise to be good."

"That's all I can ask for. That and that you don't go charging into the fray again, no matter how likely it seems that danger is imminent."

Black held up his middle and index fingers together. "Scout's honor."

She cast a sideways glance at him. "You were never a boy scout."

"I should've known better than to try and sneak that past you."

"This should be a simple assignment," she said. "We get in and out with the information. And then we're back on a plane to Washington by midnight."

"Sounds easy enough."

They came around the bend and were face to face with Dr. Becker's estate, which was surrounded by a ten-foot high wall constructed from stone. The only entrance was through a large wooden gate guarded by a pair of armed men.

"You're good to go," Hawk said. "Your photos just uploaded to the database. Congratulations. You are now Mr. and Mrs. Muncie."

"I always liked the name Angela," Alex said.

"It seems fitting with the blonde wig that you're sporting," Black said. "All the Angelas I've ever known always dyed their hair."

She glanced over at Black. "You ready?"

He nodded as they eased to a stop next to the guard station, just short of entering the grounds. The estate was an old castle that had been renovated and restored to its full glory from the late nineteenth century. The turrets on the corners of the walls were unmanned, and security seemed rather lax, at least according to the standards that Alex was used to dealing with.

While they waited for the signal to proceed, Alex combed her hair before deciding to put it up in a bun.

The guard at the gate wore a pair of white gloves and had a semi-automatic weapon slung over his shoulder. After completing a check of the vehicle in front of them, he motioned for Alex to roll down her window.

"Invitation and identification, please," he said as he held out his hand.

"Good evening," Alex said as she slid the requested documents into the man's hands. He studied them carefully before shining his flashlight inside the sports car at Alex. Crouching down to get eye level with the window, the guard lit up Black's face as well.

The guard stood upright again and then handed everything back to Alex.

"Have a good evening," he said before waving them through.

She rolled up the window and slipped inside, following the instructions of the attendant directing them toward the front door. After she came to a stop near the front steps, a pair of young men hustled around to open the car doors to Alex's vehicle. The idea of handing off the keys to a valet without a quick way of gaining access to her car was unsettling, but she'd requested two keys at the rental agency for such a moment.

"Take good care of her," Alex said as she winked at the young man who was preparing to slide into the driver's seat.

Once they were inside, a man greeted them at the door and offered to take Alex's coat, but she declined his offer. Alex and Black were ushered to walk through a metal detector, which cleared both of them. Alex smiled as she considered how easy it was to disguise their weapons from the machine.

"We're through," she said.

"Roger that," Hawk said. "You just came into view on one of the feeds I was monitoring. Give me the layout of the room."

"Two guards at each of the exits, both armed with handguns. There are obviously several cameras around the room. Other than that, just your typical nineteenth-century castle great hall."

"Do you recognize anyone?" Hawk asked.

"Not so far," Alex said. "This crowd appears rather harmless to me. I'm not sure what the real purpose of this gathering is, but I'm starting to believe it's just what it says it is: an environmental fundraiser."

Black swiped a couple of champagne glasses and handed one to Alex.

"Thank you," she said. "Such a gentleman."

"Alex, I'm beginning to think you're just messing with me," Hawk said.

"You're too easy, honey," she said. "This is quite fun for me."

"Well, you do look absolutely ravishing in that dress and coat. You appear to be quite the sophisticate with deep pockets to boot."

"Focus," Alex said. "This isn't about my blonde wig or how stunning I look tonight. We need to find Dr. Becker and keep an eye on him in order to figure out the right moment to approach him."

Guests continued to pour through the doors until the room was filled with at least sixty couples. Alex estimated the median age of the crowd was somewhere around fifty-five or sixty with a few outliers on both the younger and older side. She could tell that she and Black stood out more than she'd hoped they would, but that wasn't something she had any control over. With her makeup, she did her best to make her look like a woman in her early fifties, drawing in lines and accentuating her burgeoning crow's feet. The attempt wasn't perfect, but she certainly didn't appear to be the late twenties brunette that she was.

Alex and Black mingled, careful to introduce themselves as Angela and Phillip to the others milling around the room and sharing drinks together. Finally, after half an hour, Alex saw someone she recognized.

"I'm suddenly starting to wonder what kind of group this really is," she said.

"What do you mean?" Hawk asked over the coms.

"I just saw Jeremiah Gillman," she said. "He was one of the men listed as a client of Andrei Orlovsky's, our favorite Russian arms dealer. I remember his name and looking him up. He's got quite the resume when it comes to arrests. I doubt he's simply here to help save the planet. I know for a fact that he's more interested in destroying it."

"In that case, steer clear," Hawk said. "We don't need to stir up any more trouble that we're already going to have before this thing is said and done."

"I believe I told you that I was rather confident about everything going as planned here," Alex said. "If Gillman is our sole threat, I'm sure we'll be able to handle him."

"Just stay alert."

Alex watched the crowd sift back and forth across the room, like a listless tide. Attendees flitted from one conversation to the next, most touting what they'd been able to do in the past year to bolster their standing as a true warrior for the environment. Alex learned enough about the Muncies to know what they had done, which included starting a business reward program for employers to incentivize their people to utilize water fountains. After her fourth retelling of the story, Black offered to retell it next, which he did flawlessly.

"We make a great team," Alex said.

"Yes, we do," piped Hawk.

"I was talking about Black and me. For some reason, we just haven't fought as much as you and I do, Hawk, when we're out in the field."

"That's good to hear," Hawk said with a sarcastic chuckle. "Can you please just save the commentary until after you're all done with the operation?"

"If I didn't know any better, Hawk, I'd think you were jealous," she said.

"Can you blame me?" Hawk said. "You're dazzling tonight."

"I won't argue with that."

Black tapped Alex's shoulder with the back of his hand. "Look over there. Dr. Becker is preparing to speak."

Becker tapped a microphone and cleared his throat. "May I have your attention, please? I want to thank you all for coming tonight to this benefit. I can't tell you how much it means to me to see so many friends taking time out of your busy schedules to be here to support a cause that I feel is important for the future of our planet."

He sipped his drink before continuing.

"As you know, I've written several papers on the impact our degenerating environment is having on children, and if we don't take action now, we're going to do irreparable damage to this beautiful world that we live in. And as you all know, this message isn't one widely accepted."

"Here we go," Black said under his breath to Alex. "Can I just rush the doc right now and carry him out of here before he continues this fear-mongering speech?"

Alex glared at him. "I warned you about that. Control yourself."

"It was a joke," Black said. "I'm not going to jeopardize this mission."

Becker rambled on for another five minutes before closing with a pitch to donate to the Defenders of the Earth Society or, as he later referenced it, DOE. Alex had researched the non-profit beforehand to see Becker's level of involvement. He was easily the most prominent board member among a list of names she didn't recognize. Her attempts to dig up more information on the others resulted in dead ends. It was almost as if they didn't exist, which was curious for a group that was raising large amounts of cash.

"Okay, maybe I wasn't joking," Black said. "This is bordering on the absurd."

"Be patient," Alex said. "He's wrapping this up, and then we'll talk to him in private."

"His study is down the corridor directly behind him," Hawk said over the coms. "From what I can see, there aren't any guards patrolling that area, so you should be able to get in there without being seen."

Several guests approached Becker after his presentation, irking Alex that they got to him first. Once he was finally free, Alex looked at Black.

"Now's our chance," she said. "Time to go."

Black wove through the crowd, grabbing a drink off one of the wine trays held by a server as he went. Alex sauntered up to Becker.

"Thank you so much for inviting us," Alex said. "My husband and I are just delighted to be a part of such a wonderful organization doing so many great things for the world."

"You're welcome," Becker said, pausing as he stared blankly at Alex's face. "Remind me of your name again. I can't quite place it at the moment."

"Angela," she said. "Angela Muncie. You invited me and my husband, Phillip."

"Ah, yes," Becker said. "Please forgive me for not remembering. Events like these have a way of exposing my weak memory skills."

"All is forgiven. I was interested in making a sizeable donation, but I wanted to speak with you about it—in private."

"Of course. Just follow me this way to my office. Hopefully, that will give you all the privacy you require."

Becker led Alex down the corridor and then unlocked his office door. He gestured for her to enter and followed his lead, easing inside.

"So, what concerns do you have or questions can I answer for you?" he asked as he followed her into the room. He closed the door behind him but didn't see Black wedged between the wall and a briefcase near the far corner.

"Before I give you a dime of my money, I was wondering if you could tell me why you were meeting with an international terrorist mastermind," Alex said as she produced a picture from her clutch.

Becker's mouth fell agape as he stared at the photo of him in a café with Evana Bahar. He scowled for a moment but remained quiet.

"What's the matter, Dr. Becker? Is your memory failing you again?"

"Who are you?" he demanded.

Black jammed his gun into Becker's back. "I think the lady asked you a question. I suggest you answer it."

Becker glanced over his shoulder at Black. "You do realize you'll never get out of here alive."

"That's not the first time we've been told that," Black said. "Yet, here we are."

"What do you people want?" Becker asked as his face turned pale.

"We need to know how you contact Obsidian," Alex said.

"Contact who?"

Black used his gun barrel to apply more pressure on Becker's back. "We're through playing games, Doc. Think long and hard about what your next response is going to be."

Becker swallowed hard. "Okay, I know some people involved in the organization."

Alex furrowed her brow. "You just know some people involved? I would hope that your relationship would be stronger than acquaintances if you're partnering with them on missions."

"What are on Earth are you talking about?"

"I think you know exactly what I'm talking about," Alex said. "Six months ago you were in New York at the U.N. building when a bomber slipped inside and threatened to kill everyone. There was the threat of a virus, but you found a way out of the building and took something with you, too."

"You must have me mistaken for someone else, I never—"

She wagged her finger at Becker. "Would you like

to see the video from that day where you slipped through the barricade and escaped into the city streets?"

After opening her phone, Alex scrolled to the video of Becker weaving his way through the crowd and breaking free before hustling down the street.

"Obviously you weren't infected," Black said. "But you took something out of there. What was it?"

"Look, I don't know what it was," Becker said. "I was just a courier, doing a favor for a friend."

"You're lying," she said.

Black jammed his gun a little harder into Becker's back.

"It's the truth, I swear it," Becker said.

Alex narrowed her eyes. "How do you contact them?"

"I don't. They contact me."

"How do you contact them?" she said.

Becker just glared back at her.

"The lady's not gonna ask you a third time," Black said.

Becker sighed. "I have a phone in the top drawer of my desk that's used exclusively for contacting them."

Alex strode over to the desk and retrieved the mobile. She held it out in front of Becker.

"Password, please."

He typed in the digits. "You don't know how powerful these people are. They'll hunt you down and kill you—and do it all before breakfast."

"We've heard it all before," Alex said, "yet, here I am. So, let's get moving."

Black shoved Becker to his chair and bound him to it with several zip ties.

"Thanks for inviting us tonight," Black said. "You throw a great party."

Alex opened the door and gestured for Black to hurry up. He went ahead of her down the hallway, tucking his gun discreetly into the back of his pants as he went.

"We've secured the package," Alex said over the coms.

"Nice work," Hawk said. "Now get the hell out of there before he alerts security."

"Oh, I doubt he'll be doing anything of the sort for quite some time," Black said.

Alex and Black slipped through the crowd still milling around in the great hall. Once they reached the front door, they encountered the lead valet, who requested their ticket.

"That's okay," Alex said as she pushed her way past him. "We'll get it ourselves."

"Ma'am, I'm afraid I can't let you do that," he said. "We must get the cars for you. You don't even know where it is."

Alex and Black continued walking, ignoring his pleas for them to wait.

"I said stop," the valet said, followed by the sound of him chambering a round into his gun.

Alex and Black spun around to see the valet with a weapon trained on them. They both threw their hands in the air in surrender.

"I'm just going to reach inside my purse here and get it for you," Alex said, moving very slowly.

She retrieved with her fingertips and held it up for the valet. He walked up to her and yanked it out of her hands.

"Wait on the sidewalk like everyone else," he said.

Alex and Black followed the command while the valet radioed one of his underlings to retrieve the car for them.

"This should only take a minute—and then you can be on your way," the valet said.

Alex and Black remained silent as they stood still at the edge of the curb awaiting their car to appear. After a couple minutes, the car roared around the corner and then halted in front of them. The valet opened the passenger door for Alex. However, when Black walked around to get in the driver's side, the man driving the car got out with his weapon trained on Black.

"You're not going anywhere," the man said. "Both of you need to follow me."

"What the hell is going on?" Hawk squawked into their earpieces. "Are you guys all right?"

"There's nothing quite like getting ambushed by your valet," Alex said, doing her best to disguise her communication with Hawk.

He let out a string of expletives before begging them to remain calm and be patient. "I'm on my way."

"Let's pick up the pace," the guard said. "We don't have all night—and Dr. Becker is looking forward to having another conversation with you two."

CHAPTER 8

ALEX STARED AT THE WALLS as she descended a series of staircases with Black and wondered just how long the castle had been here. Intricate stonework decorated the interior, equivalent to the kind of craftsmanship she'd seen in dozens of European fortresses. The only sign that she hadn't been transported back in time were the security cameras perched high along the corridor and the modern weapons slung around the necks of the guards escorting their prisoners below ground.

"I don't know about you," Black said, "but I'm half expecting us to see a dragon chained up down here."

Alex smiled and shook her head. "And here I thought I was the one breathing fire when the doc tried to lie to us."

When they reached the end of the hallway, the guards slung Black and Alex into a cell and locked the gate. The men strode away without giving their captives even a second glance.

"Well, I guess we know what's coming next," she said.

"Yeah, and it ain't gonna be pretty," Black said.

"Can you two talk?" Hawk asked, interrupting over the comlinks.

"For now," Alex said. "I guess they didn't see our coms."

"We'll just be grateful for our good fortune and go from there," Hawk said. "As long as they're working, I should be able to locate you and get you both the hell outta there."

"I'd act quickly," Alex said. "We haven't seen Dr. Becker yet—and I still have his cell phone."

"It's probably how he tracked us down," Black said. "You should've turned it off."

"It's too late now," she said. "There's nothing we can do about it at this point."

"Don't I know that all too well," Black said. "That's the story of my life."

Alex sighed and slumped to the floor, resting against the back wall. Black joined her, sitting down a few feet away.

"What exactly is the story of your life?" Alex asked. "You know since we have all the time to kill."

Black nodded. "We've got all the time in the world, don't we?"

"Not if I have anything to say about it," Hawk

said over the coms. "Just hang in there, you two."

"We're not going anywhere in the foreseeable future," she said before turning toward Black. "Now where were we? Ah, yes, at the very beginning."

Black chuckled softly. "This is the point of the story where everything starts off bad and you think things can only get better. But that's not the case. It's one horrible and awful thing after another. And to be honest, I'm not sure this is the kind of story that will keep our spirits up while we wait for Hawk."

"Beats watching the mice over there scurry back and forth across the floor in search of food."

"In that case, let me back up and start about two months before I was born," Black said. "My father was deployed overseas, flying A-10s in the Gulf War, while my mother was pregnant with me and living in Tucson. He got caught up in some ground fire on a mission over Iraq and had to parachute out when he lost both engines. Unfortunately, he was captured by some members of Saddam Hussein's Republican Guard and dragged through the streets before dying."

Alex winced as Black continued his story.

"That left me without a father for the first six years of my life. My mother eventually remarried a man from my father's squadron, but he was messed up. He drank a lot and beat my mother nightly. One night when I was twelve years old, he came home drunk and reeking of perfume. My mother confronted him about his whereabouts, and they got into a huge argument. The next thing I knew, he pulled out a gun and shot my mother before killing himself."

"That's more than any person should have to endure," she said, fighting back tears.

"I'm not done yet," Black said, shaking his head. "I was placed into the foster care system when my grandparents declined to take me. But that wasn't a great experience for me either as my foster father beat me and verbally abused me quite often. Needless to say, I had a lot of pent up anger, which I figured out that I needed to express in a way that didn't result in me getting into fights weekly at school. So I started playing football."

"Running back?" she asked.

"Linebacker. I loved obliterating receivers across the middle of the field. My nickname was 'The Hit Man'."

"And now you are one," she said.

"It didn't start out that way," Black continued. "I was offered a college scholarship to play at Notre Dame, but my grades weren't good enough. So I went to junior college and had every intention of getting my transcript in order and earning an associate's degree so I could transfer and play again, but then life happened again. I was attending a school in Kansas in the middle of nowhere and was at our local Walmart one night with my girlfriend Lana when a deranged lunatic walked in with a gun. He started shooting anyone that moved. I wanted to get out of there, so we ran toward the back, but it was locked. The shooter was a disgruntled employee who had planned out his massacre. As I was searching for another way out, he came up behind us and gave me this sadistic grin before pulling the trigger. I stepped in front of Lana and pulled her close to me as we dove to the side. However, he sprinted after us and shot her in the head first before turning his gun on me. I shoved the barrel away and kicked him backward before scrambling down the aisle. He fired a shot that hit me in my shoulder blade, but I kept running. I went for the gun section and grabbed a rifle off the shelf and started loading. The only good thing my foster father ever did was to teach me how to shoot a gun. I pulled out a nearby ladder used to retrieve items stored high behind the counter and climbed up so I could see almost the entire floor. Once I saw where that lunatic was, I scoped him in and picked him off. That scumbag still had several rounds of ammunition draped over his neck. He only killed eight people including Lana, but there's no telling how many more would've died if he hadn't been stopped. The next day, a man from the CIA paid me a visit—and here I am."

"Whoa," Alex said. "That's heavy. I'm so sorry you had to go through all that."

Black sighed. "It wasn't the ideal childhood, but it did help shape me into the man that I am today."

"I just can't believe you're so well adjusted."

Black laughed softly. "Looks can be deceiving."

"Hawk, are you still there?" Alex asked.

"I'm about five minutes out," Hawk said. "Any change in your status?"

"We're still down here in the dungeon and alone at the moment."

"Roger that."

The door at the end of the corridor creaked as it flung open. A quartet of guards entered and strode toward them.

"Check that," Alex said. "We have company. Four of them."

"Roger that," Hawk said.

Once the men reached the front of Alex's and Black's cell, a guard hastily unlocked it and yanked the gate open. The other men stormed inside and began beating both Alex and Black. The punching and kicking lasted no more than a minute, brought to an end by the entrance of Dr. Becker into the room.

"That's enough," Becker said.

Alex was on her hands and knees, blood dripping from the corner of her mouth. She wiped it with the back of her hand as she rose to her feet.

"I didn't tell you to stand, did I?" Becker said before sweeping his leg behind Alex and sending back to the floor.

He circled them in silence with his arms crossed. Alex wanted to give him a piece of her mind, but she was aching all over and preferred to avoid any more physical combat.

I wish I had a gun about now.

* * *

DR. BECKER WASN'T USED to having his home descended upon by foreign agents, though it had happened before—once. Becker was beaten and nearly left for dead during a scrappy fight in the great hall. The fracas came to an abrupt end when he was being pinned down near the fireplace, and he managed to grab a poker and impale his attacker. That was the last day he didn't employ at least four full-time security guards.

Despite the Americans' best efforts to disguise themselves, Becker knew that they weren't the Muncies. The facial recognition camera had told his staff as much when Alex and Black walked through the door. But Becker was curious about their identities and what their reason was for being here, allowing them to proceed unimpeded for most of the night. However, when they tried to get away with his phone to contact Obsidian, he decided it was time to not only take his phone back but also to send a message to whoever was handling them. The phone didn't really matter since every week a new number was assigned as well as a new device to call her on. But it was the principle of the situation that mattered to Becker. He was going to right a few wrongs. No longer was he pretending to be the scared and meek scientist.

Becker narrowed his eyes and set his jaw. "How dare you enter my house and make demands of me. You're only alive because I wanted to see what you were up to. Now, it's time for payback."

Becker whipped a cropping stick from his belt and pounded it into his left hand while continuing to circle his captives.

"So, any volunteers for who would like to go first?"

He looked down at them, and neither was responding, let alone moving.

"In that case, I'll choose Mrs. Muncie."

She mumbled something that he couldn't make out. He knelt down next to her.

"What was that, Mrs. Muncie?" he asked again.

"I said, I can't hear you." She curled up into a fetal position, covering her head with her arms and almost disappearing.

Before Becker could respond, a piercing pain resonated in his ears. He staggered to the ground and gritted his teeth to fight through the pain.

CHAPTER 9

ALEX KNEW WHAT THE NOISE was as she'd tested it on herself in the Phoenix Foundation lab one day when assessing the device's usefulness. The ear-splitting sound emanating from the tiny box was something Hawk had deployed in an effort to make his extraction mission run more smoothly. She raised her head to see him running down the corridor, firing shot after shot at the guards. When all four crumpled to the ground, Hawk flung a canister of smoke in her direction.

She knew what he was doing, creating a smokescreen in case reinforcements entered at the opposite end of the hallway. But he didn't see Becker still trying to fight through the noise.

"Becker's still alive," she warned over their coms. But it was a pointless plea. The high-pitched blast rendered their coms useless.

She looked over at Black, whose hands were cupped tightly against his ears. He grimaced as he looked back at her.

Staying on the ground, Alex heard the sounds of bodies dropping to the floor. Counting them as they fell, she was concerned when the number stopped with four. She glanced around and saw Becker refusing to succumb to the ear-splitting sound.

Alex strained to see through the smoke that had now wafted throughout the corridor, making it difficult to see in either direction. Seconds later, the gas cleared away enough that she could make out Hawk's silhouette down the hallway. She nodded toward the opposite doorway, gesturing the direction they needed to go. While pointing would've made it so much easier, she wasn't about to remove her hands from the side of her head for even a second.

Hawk gave her a subtle nod, and she started to run toward him. However, she didn't go more a few feet before she felt herself getting pulled backward. Spinning around to see what was holding her up, she noticed Becker's hand clutching a fistful of her shirt. Black didn't hesitate to help, lowering his shoulder and ramming Becker against the wall. But he didn't relinquish his grip that easily and slammed Alex into the hard stone also.

Becker tried to train his weapon on Black, but Alex jerked back and forth, making it impossible for the scientist to steady his hand to get a good shot. He fired anyway, the bullet ricocheting off the ceiling.

Alex delivered a solid kick to Becker's midsection, enabling her to get free of his grip.

Almost all of the smoke had evaporated, and Hawk was only a few meters away. She turned and ran toward him, praying that Becker wouldn't be able to get a shot off. As she looked ahead, she noticed Hawk sprinting with his gun aiming just to the left of her head. He squeezed off two rounds.

Alex shot a final glance over her shoulder to see what happened to Becker, but he was gone. Hawk grabbed her hand and told her to run, while he backpedaled with his weapon, ready to fire if Becker reappeared around the corner.

The crippling sound device ended, allowing them to speak to one another for the first time.

"We have to move quickly," Hawk said. "There are more guards out there, and they will pin us down if we aren't careful."

"We need to take Becker with us," Alex said. "He knows what's really going on."

"No," Hawk said. "I'm nixing that idea."

"This is our chance, Hawk. He's obviously not just some low-level delivery boy like he wanted us to believe. My gut tells me that whatever Obsidian is up to, Becker is playing a pivotal role in it all."

"We don't have time," Hawk said. "We need to go now."

"But Hawk—"

Hawk grabbed Alex's arm. "Now."

She huffed as she withdrew from his grasp before spinning toward the door. As she looked down, she noticed a cell phone lying on the ground, the same one she'd swiped from Becker earlier. Alex knelt down and picked it up.

"Come on, Alex," Hawk said. "This is deadly serious."

"I'm coming," she said with a growl.

* * *

WHEN THE GUARDS started dropping, Becker knew he was in for a fight. But he underestimated the ability of the American operative to storm his castle without any idea about its layout and successfully extract a pair of prisoners.

The bullet that tore through his left bicep was painful and needed immediate attention, but he wasn't going to let his captives escape that easily. He hustled around the corner to get out of harm's way and slumped against the wall. Glancing down at his bloodied arm, he gritted his teeth and winced as his arm felt like it was on fire. After ripping off part of his shirttail, he tied the piece around the wound to ensure constant pressure was being applied.

He radioed the head of security to give him an update and to make sure that the gate was still closed.

"Don't let anyone leave the grounds," Becker said.

"I only have two men with me," the security chief said. "Where are the four I sent you?"

Becker looked at one of the men still writhing on the ground, groaning as he couldn't stop the bleeding from a gunshot wound.

"They're gone," Becker said.

"All of them?"

"Yeah." Becker knew he could save the man in front of him, but the result would be the prisoners escaping. And Becker wasn't about to let that happen.

"Help me," moaned the other guard.

Becker closed his eyes and looked away.

To hell with my oath.

Becker slowly rose to his feet before hustling back to the security office to see about getting a better idea of his guests were.

Then he stopped and froze, checking his pants pockets for the cell phone. It was gone.

I must've dropped it in the cell.

He didn't have any time to lament the loss of the phone. Once he caught the couple posing as the Muncies, he would have the cell back in his possession soon enough. He'd also have the opportunity to find out just who these people were and what they were doing crashing his fundraiser.

At the security office, he talked strategy with the chief before scanning all the monitors.

"Where was the last place you saw them?" Becker asked.

"They were in the wine cellar, sir."

"And most of the guests are still here?"

"They noticed a slight commotion when several of the guards left, but no one seems to be too concerned."

"Let's hope it stays that way."

Becker started checking the screens. They weren't anywhere to be found.

Where did you go?

"Lock down the gate," Becker said to his security chief. "Inspect every vehicle thoroughly before it leaves the grounds. Let the guards know we're looking for two men and a woman. And share still images with the remaining guards so they know who they're looking for."

* * *

HAWK HOISTED HIMSELF onto the veranda using the stone fencing surrounding the area. A man stood outside alone, leaning on the railing as he smoked a cigar. When he noticed Hawk, he dropped his glass tumbler, shattering it on the ground.

Hawk put his index finger to his lips and gestured for the man to move into the shadows.

"Do you have a car?" Hawk asked.

"What on Earth is this all about?" the man asked with widening eyes.

Hawk brandished his weapon. "Do you have a car?"

"I drove here with my wife," he said. "Why do you ask?"

"Because you're going to help me and my friends get out of here. Go ask the valet for your car."

"Why would I do that?"

"We need to leave, and you're going to drive us out of here."

"What if I refuse?" the man asked.

"I have a partner inside right now. We know what your wife looks like. All I have to do is say the word and your wife won't go home with you tonight."

"You're bluffing," the man said with a sneer.

Hawk glanced at his gun. "You sure you want to take that chance?"

The man sighed. "Let me get my wife."

"I'll meet you out front," Hawk said. "Five minutes. Don't be late."

Hawk climbed back over the railing and shimmied down to the ground where Alex and Black were waiting.

"Once the old man I found requests his car, go ask for yours," Hawk said. "That will clear out the other valet and make it easy for us to get into the car."

"Don't you think they'll be expecting us out front?" Alex asked.

"Maybe, but there aren't many guards left, and they're going to scouring the grounds for us," Hawk said. "With a guard at the gate, I'm banking on them expecting us to go over the wall somehow."

"I hope you're right," Alex said.

"This is definitely our best move," Black said.

Hawk and Black connected with a quick fist bump before they crept along in the shadows. Once they reached the front, the old man was there with his wife. He handed his ticket to one of the attendants and waited on the steps. Meanwhile, Hawk followed the valet into the underground garage and then ambushed him, easing up behind him and putting him in a headlock. In a matter of seconds, he went to sleep. Hawk pressed the key fob, activating the car's horn to locate the old man's vehicle. He pulled around to the front, surprising the man again when he stepped from behind the steering wheel and opened the door for him.

Once the man and his wife got in, Alex slid into the backseat, while Hawk and Black piled into the trunk. Hawk poked the armrest forward just far enough that he could hear everything taking place in the front.

"Just stay calm," Hawk said. "We'll be out of your lives in just a few minutes."

"I will," the old man said. "Don't worry."

They rolled to a stop just outside the gate and were greeted by a guard. He wore a scowl along with a semi-automatic weapon slung around his neck as he lumbered toward them.

"Did you have a nice time at the party?" the guard asked.

"Fine time, sir," the old man said.

"If you had such a fine time, why are you leaving so soon?" the guard asked. "You're the first guests to leave."

"I have an early flight tomorrow morning."

"Would you mind letting me check the trunk?" the guard asked.

"Be my guest," the old man said without flinching. However, he didn't pop the trunk. Instead, he just sat there with the car idling.

"Sir," the guard called, "I need you to open the trunk so I can inspect it."

The old man didn't move.

"It's okay," Hawk said. "Do what he says. We can handle ourselves."

Hawk trained his gun upward and waited for the trunk to swing open.

CHAPTER 10

HAWK STARED UPWARD and tried to think two moves ahead once he eliminated the guard. The gunfire was sure to draw attention and send what remaining security force Dr. Becker had running toward the entrance. Hawk decided that kicking the trunk open could surprise the guard and knock him out before any weapons went off.

As a result, Hawk recoiled his legs, pressing his feet against the top of the trunk and waiting for the lock to click free. Hawk had already plotted out what to do next and mentioned the next course of action to Black.

"You good?" Hawk asked.

"Roger that," Black said.

Hawk swallowed hard as he heard the sound of the guard fingering the latch. The trunk barely moved an inch before Hawk thrust his feet upward, slamming the metal into the guard's face. He staggered sideways before Hawk caught the man with two hits, one to the throat and the other to the face. Before he had a chance to fight back, he collapsed to the ground, out cold.

The old man shifted into gear and stepped on the gas while Hawk was still dragging the guard's body into the station.

Alex cocked her gun. "What do you think you're doing?"

The man stomped on the brakes and waited for Hawk, who joined Black in the backseat.

Packed tightly inside, they shifted from side to side as the old man wove down the winding road leading away from the castle.

"You don't need to drive so fast," Alex said. "There's no one right behind us."

"I'm not slowing down for anything. They're probably already after us."

"You need to slow down up ahead because that's our van," she said.

He growled as he eased off the accelerator and tapped the brakes. Once the car came to a stop, he popped the trunk, sending Hawk and Black scrambling out of it.

"Thank you, sir," Hawk said.

The old man flashed a rude gesture before stomping on the gas and speeding away.

"Time to get home and figure out what's really

going on," Hawk said.

The team piled into the van and was tearing down the mountainside seconds later.

* * *

THE NEXT EVENING, Blunt welcomed the team home at the Phoenix Foundation offices, convening to discuss what they gleaned on their visit to Switzerland. Hawk nursed a cup of coffee as he settled into his chair next to Alex.

"Trying to wake up?" Blunt asked.

Hawk shook his head subtly. "It's been a long thirty-six hours. I still haven't recovered."

"All that time on the plane and you didn't catch up on your sleep?"

Black walked into the meeting and sat down across from Hawk and Alex as Blunt finished his comment.

"No matter how tired you are," Black began, "it's difficult to settle down after an operation like that. At least, I know it is for me."

"Well, you're all awake enough to be here, and it's time to talk about what you found at Dr. Becker's fundraiser," Blunt said.

Alex opened up her laptop. "I couldn't sleep on the flight home either, so I started working on the phone we lifted off Dr. Becker."

"Was it encrypted?" Blunt asked.

Alex nodded. "Yes, but I managed to crack it just

before we touched down. Whoever is running Obsidian has some advanced technology. I couldn't get a geolocation on any of the numbers dialed from this phone. They were essentially all phony numbers."

"How can that be?" Blunt asked.

She shrugged. "I've read about some software that can do this while visiting the dark web, but I've never come across it."

"So, the phone is a dead end, just like the trip," Blunt said.

"Only if Becker warned his Obsidian contact," she said. "But according to him, this was the only way they communicated, and it was always a one-way communication."

"So, what are you saying?" Blunt asked.

"I'm saying we have a way to contact Obsidian."

Blunt slapped the table and grinned. "How long will it take you to set up a way to get a bead on their location if we call them tonight?"

"Maybe half an hour," Alex said.

"Great," Blunt said. "We'll meet back here in thirty minutes."

For the next few minutes, Alex worked hard to get all her programs set up to track the number, while Hawk and Black finished their reports from the operation. When she finished, she called everyone back to the room.

"Hawk," she said, "I think you should be the one to do the honors."

Hawk sighed and took the phone in his hands. He looked up slowly at Alex.

"Just hit the redial button," Alex said. "Hopefully we'll get some answers."

He followed Alex's instructions and waited patiently as the phone rang. Three times, then four. Still nothing. A fifth and sixth ring. Nobody had answered yet. But just as the phone was about to ring a seventh time—and Hawk was about to hang up—a man replied on the other end.

"I was wondering what was taking you so long to give me a call, Mr. Hawk," the man said.

There was a long, pregnant pause. Hawk said nothing as he glanced around the room at his colleagues.

"This is Mr. Hawk, isn't it?" the man asked.

"Yes, and who is this?" Hawk asked.

"Your mother swore you would find me, though I am surprised it took you so long. I was beginning to wonder if she mattered as much to you and we believed."

Hawk felt his heart begin to race. In the midst of dealing with the pain of losing his mother, he figured it had to be from some terrorist operative he battled in the past. Maybe a grieving brother set on getting his pound of flesh. Or a disgruntled arms dealer who had his operation ruined by one of Hawk's missions. But someone with a connection to Obsidian? Hawk hadn't even considered that. Obsidian seemed to operate at a different level, and this attack underscored it. They decided to confront a man who could be the fly in their ointment instead of letting him disrupt their plans later on down the line.

"Just keep him talking," Alex whispered. "I'm getting close to finding his location."

"What do you want with me?" Hawk asked the man.

"The same thing I wanted with your mother—I want you dead. You're a difficult man to find, Mr. Hawk."

"There are other ways to get my attention."

"I've found it's challenging to get people's attention sometimes. But nothing seems to work like killing their mother."

"You're one sick bastard."

Alex looked at Hawk and gestured with her hand for him keep talking.

"I've been called worse."

"I thought Obsidian was better connected," Hawk said. "Surely you could've found me another way."

"Good luck finding me, Mr. Hawk. I'll be waiting."

The line went dead. Alex pounded her fist on the table.

"I'm assuming you didn't get his location?" Hawk asked.

She shook her head. "I was so close. He obviously knew what he was doing and was just toying with us.

"Now what?" Hawk asked. "Can't you glean anything from that?"

"I can run his voice through a database and see if I can find something, but it's still not going to tell us where he is."

"Maybe we can figure out where he is some other way. He wants me to find him."

"Yeah," Alex said, "but he doesn't want to make it easy on you. Makes you wonder why Obsidian is so intent on distracting you."

"Maybe he can tell us," Hawk said.

"Or maybe it'll be too late," Black suggested.

"Too late for what?" Hawk asked.

"For whatever Obsidian is planning."

CHAPTER 11

THE NEXT MORNING, Blunt called the team together to discuss their next steps. He didn't doubt Alex's skills at pinpointing Becker's Obsidian contact, but he did wonder if a good night of sleep in their own beds might be just what they all needed to regain their edge.

Hawk and Alex filed into the room behind Black, who was drinking a cup of coffee. Blunt noted how they all still seemed exhausted.

"I hope everyone slept well last night," Blunt said.

"My sleep has been pretty restless ever since those animals murdered my mother," Hawk said. "That won't change until we catch the man who did this."

"We'll find him," Blunt said. "But we can't lose sight of the bigger picture at this point. It's apparent that Obsidian is preparing to make a big move and wants to eliminate any speed bumps along the way."

"And Hawk is the speed bump?" Alex asked. "It's like they don't even know about Black here."

"I'm sure they do," Blunt said, "and they probably have a plan for him as well. They just haven't tipped their hand yet."

"Or maybe they're hoping to get a two-for-one special," Black said. "They think they can take out both of us at the same time."

"They very well could," Blunt said. "That's why it's imperative for us to be so vigilant right now. If we hear or see anything, we can't ignore it. We must be ready for any scenario."

Alex shook her head. "The scenario we're all dealing with right now is that we have no credible leads. That number we called was rerouted so many times I lost count. I'm at a loss for any other ways to find his location."

Blunt pulled out a cigar and snipped the end off before jamming it into his mouth. He chewed on the tobacco for a few seconds before responding. "Do you have a recording of that phone call you can play for us again?"

Alex nodded and opened her laptop.

"Can you play it over the speakers in the room?" he asked. "I thought I heard something while he was speaking, and it bugged me all last night."

Alex pounded on her keyboard and after a few

seconds looked up at Blunt.

"I'm ready whenever you are," she said.

"Let's have a listen."

The original recording boomed over the sound system. Blunt glanced at Hawk, who winced again when the Obsidian agent bragged about killing Hawk's mother. Hawk clenched his fists and shifted in his chair.

With eyes darting back and forth while looking upward, Blunt concentrated on the conversation. There was something he swore he'd heard in the background—then, he was confident he heard it again.

"Stop it right there," Blunt said. "Can you back that up just a few seconds?"

Alex complied and replayed the conversation from that point.

"Okay. Pause it," Blunt said before Alex tapped her computer and halted the clip. "Can you isolate the background noise?"

"You think you hear something distinct?" Black asked.

Blunt nodded. "It feels like a long shot, but I haven't been able to get it out of my mind. I just need to know for sure before we move on."

"Give me a second," Alex said as her fingers went to work.

Blunt put on his reading glasses and studied some of his files on Obsidian while Alex fulfilled her boss's request.

"Ready?" Alex asked as she leaned back in her chair.

Blunt removed his spectacles and nodded. She tapped a key and the recording resumed, this time with the exchange between Hawk and the agent barely audible. Alex had enhanced the ambient noise, much to Blunt's delight.

"Good job," he whispered as he listened.

Midway through the recording, Blunt heard what he was listening for, the smooth baritone voice of auctioneer Charlie Bell. Blunt clapped his hands and pointed at Alex.

"That's it," he said. "That's exactly what I thought I heard."

Alex stopped the playback. "What did you hear?"

"That voice belongs to one of the best auctioneers at the Fort Worth Stockyard," Blunt said. "Once you see Charlie Bell in action and hear his voice, you'll never forget it. He talks a hundred miles an hour while raising bids for a longhorn and then has you spellbound with his mesmerizing description of the next animal. It's truly an art form."

"And you're sure that's him?" Alex asked.

Blunt nodded. "Charlie's style and sound are so

unique it's nearly impossible to mistake someone else for him. Charlie has been there for years, and I make it a point to go visit the stockyards in Fort Worth every time I go back if anything just to hear him auction off a few steers."

"So, now we know where he was when we called—or at least, we think we do," Hawk said. "Any way we can find out who he is?"

"I have an idea," Alex said.

"Let's hear it," Blunt said.

"Since we know the exact time of the conversation, if we could get a look at the security video from the event, we might be able to pick him out of the crowd."

"You think it'll be that easy?" Blunt asked.

She shook her head. "At this point, it's all we've got. But we should be able to isolate the Obsidian agent pretty quickly by watching for him to answer his phone at the exact moment Hawk placed the call."

"Make it happen," Blunt said.

"There is a problem with all this," Alex said. "We'll need to get a warrant to obtain all the footage from the stockyard. I doubt they're just going to hand it over unless you have some contacts down there."

Blunt sighed. "I'm not exactly a favorite of the stockyard's CEO."

"I'm sure there's a story here you need to share,"

Hawk said. "Maybe a burned bridge or two?"

"More like scorched earth," Blunt said. "Hank Wilson, who is the CEO there now, ran against me for my Senate seat one term. I obliterated the guy and exposed both of his mistresses, much to the surprise of his loyal wife."

Alex's eyes widened. "He had two mistresses?"

"Probably more, but that's what the private investigator came up within just over two weeks of tailing him," Blunt said. "The whole scandal ended his political career as well as his marriage. The crazy thing is we were hunting buddies before that. Now, I'm pretty sure he'd try to shoot me in the back if we went out hunting together."

"In that case, do we have an alternative to a warrant?" Alex asked.

"What about the NSA?" Hawk asked. "We could always see about getting the footage from them."

"The problem with that is that Obsidian is embedded everywhere," Blunt said. "Frankly, we don't know who to trust anymore."

"We can trust Mallory Kauffman," Hawk said. "Can't we, Alex?"

She nodded. "If we ever need a favor, I can always count on her."

"One day you're going to have to repay all those favors, aren't you?" Blunt asked.

"That day is not today," she said. "I'll grab my coat, and we'll go pay her a visit."

"Not now," Blunt said. "We need to wait until after hours. It's important that we avoid taking any chances that someone on the Obsidian payroll will see you. Have Ms. Kauffman meet you in the lobby after hours and escort you inside using fake identities. We can't have any record of you being there, both for your sake and for hers."

"Roger that," Alex said as she stood.

"We're so close," Blunt said. "It's past time for whoever murdered Hawk's mother to pay."

CHAPTER 12

ALEX EASED UP TO THE guard gate and rolled down her window. She collected all her credentials from the passenger seat and handed them to the armed man standing just outside. Reacting so quickly, he didn't even have an opportunity to make his demands known, a move Alex made to give off the impression that she belonged and didn't require further questioning.

"Everything looks in order, Ms. North," he said as he offered the documents back to Alex.

"Thank you," she said as she retrieved the items.

"The visitor's lot is ahead and to your left," he said. "You'll see the sign."

"Thank you, sir," she said before accelerating into the complex.

Alex glanced at the Homeland Security badge she'd created. Georgia North was her name, a low-level director with full clearance. There was something about hacking her own government's website and planting information that made her feel anxious. But she was certain she'd exercised the proper protocol to get her alias in the system. The way in which she breezed through the security checkpoint should have given her the confidence she needed to move forward without a second thought. However, the nagging feeling that she was about to get caught wouldn't go away.

After she reached out to Mallory, Alex decided that in order to keep Black and Hawk in the loop, she needed to use their coms. Any cell phone conversations were sure to be picked up by the NSA—or at least there was a great chance of that happening. But the secure channels utilized by their coms prohibited any eavesdropping. More importantly, with Mallory making a risky move to help, Alex didn't want to jeopardize her friend's standing with her superiors.

Mallory was waiting in the lobby when Alex entered.

"It's good to see you," Mallory said.

"Likewise," Alex said before greeting Mallory with a hug. "You ready to get to work?"

"Just as soon as Tom over here determines that we're not miscreants," Mallory said, nodding toward the security checkpoint.

A barrel-chested guard poked his head around

the side of the metal detector and flashed a wide grin at Mallory before giving her a friendly wave.

"Come on over, ladies," he said. "There isn't a line."

"You dating this guy?" Alex asked in a whisper.

"No, but he's a big flirt," Mallory answered. "I just play along so he likes me. You can never have enough friends around here, especially for moments just like this one."

They strode toward the machine and placed all their belongings into a small tray on the conveyor belt. Once Tom signaled for them to walk through the detector, Mallory went first followed by Alex. They retrieved their items on the other side.

"Just wait right there," Tom said to Mallory. "I need to make sure your friend has clearance."

He hustled over to a nearby computer terminal and started typing on the keyboard.

"When did they start adding in this extra protocol for checking in?" Alex asked, keeping her voice low.

"Just a couple of weeks ago," Mallory said. "Our director has been here about five years—and from what everyone else is telling me, that's about how long you have to work here before you become extremely paranoid."

"It didn't take you that long. You were paranoid

after about a week."

"Give or take a week," Mallory quipped. "I honestly think I became wary of everyone by lunch my first day on the job."

"And look where it's gotten you," Alex said with a wink.

"Yes, sneaking in agents from fellow organizations because none of us trust the ones we work for."

"Isn't that how Washington has always worked?"

"That's been my experience."

Tom prevented the conversation from going any further as he sauntered back over to the women.

"Ms. North, I'm going to let you through for now, but I had some problems pulling up your file. Have you worked with Homeland Security for long?"

"At least a couple of weeks," Alex said. "My boss told me it would take a few days for the system to update, which is why I contacted her. We're old friends. I just wanted to get familiar with what she does here and how we can coordinate our efforts while I'm at Homeland Security."

"Of course," Tom said. "I just couldn't verify your position with the department."

"Would you mind checking again?" Alex asked. "I know I'm in there."

"Certainly," Tom said with a wink before

returning to his terminal.

Once he was out of earshot, Alex activated her coms. "Hey, fellas. I need some help. And based on the problem, I think Black is more suited for the task at hand."

"What do you need?" Black asked.

"I'm getting hung up here at NSA in the lobby by Deputy Dudley Do-Right. For some reason, my picture and other information hasn't populated yet to the system, and I need this guard to verify me before he'll let me through."

"On it," Black said.

"I left everything open on my computer," she said.

"I see it," Black said. "This should only take a minute."

"We don't have a minute," Alex said. "I need it thirty seconds ago."

"Roger that."

Alex heard the whir of Black's fingers tapping out keystrokes. Thirty seconds later, he declared victory.

"Done," he said. "I republished the update, and it went through when I checked it."

Alex sighed with relief before glancing over toward Tom, who wore a confused look on his face followed by one of surprise. He abruptly got up and walked over to them.

"Well, I apologize for the holdup, ladies," Tom said. "That was really strange. Your profile and clearance level wasn't there and then—boom!—it appeared out of nowhere. You're both good to go."

"Thank you," Alex said.

"You're quite welcome," Black said.

"You're welcome," Tom called.

"That was for the security guard," Alex said in a whisper to Black. "You just stay on the line in case I need you again."

"We're not going anywhere," he replied.

Once they reached Mallory's office, she ushered Alex inside.

"This is new," Alex said as she glanced around. "When did you get these new digs?"

"I got a few perks with my latest promotion," she said. "The pay raise was nice, but not compared to having my own space. Working on the floor next to other analysts was really depressing sometimes. It's nice to be able to spread out and not worry about people bothering me."

"And that doesn't happen now that you're a supervisor?"

"Not as much as you might think. Most of my subordinates are all trying to impress me and won't bring me anything until they've verified it six ways from Sunday."

"Sounds like you've got a nice setup."

Mallory nodded. "I do indeed. Now, let's get to work on your request."

She gestured for Alex to sit down on the chair in the corner, which she pulled up next to Mallory's terminal.

"Where do we need to start?" Mallory asked.

"I need to look at some security feeds from the Fort Worth Stockyards last night."

"And you think I have that kind of access?" Mallory asked.

"Well, I thought—"

Mallory flashed a wry smile and a wink. "Of course, I do. All auction houses on U.S. soil are monitored due to the ease through which illegally obtained goods can be sold and transported. And stockyards aren't an exception. You'd be surprised at how many drug runners we've caught selling off steers who were carrying bags of heroin and cocaine. Apparently, four stomachs make it easy to mask and store drugs."

"Who knew," Alex said.

"I bet you didn't think you were going to learn that little gem when you woke up this morning, did you?"

Alex shook her head. "That's quite disturbing."

"Welcome to my world," Mallory said as she

hammered away on the keyboard. "Now, what exactly are we looking for?"

"We want to identify the man who spoke with Hawk last night. He's an Obsidian agent, and I have the exact timeframe of the call."

"Lay it on me."

Alex slipped Mallory a piece of paper that contained the exact second the call was picked up, the length of the conversation, and a USB drive with a recording of the man's voice.

"Quite thorough," Mallory said.

"We need to find this guy as soon as possible."

Mallory entered some of the search parameters into her program and let it run. There were six men who answered their phones at the exact same moment as the Obsidian operative. One by one, Mallory and Alex eliminated them based on the length of the call until there were only two remaining.

"We're running out of options," Mallory said.

Alex shifted in her seat. "Just keep going."

They tracked the next man's phone call, and it matched perfectly.

"Well, we've got at least one," Mallory said as she captured the man's face and dropped it into a recognition search program. Then she started working on the lone remaining man. She went through the footage and found that the two men hung up at the exact same moment as well.

"Now we have two," Mallory said.

The first man's image came up in the database as a rancher from just outside of Fort Worth. His rap sheet consisted of only a handful of speeding tickets.

"He looks like a veritable Boy Scout," Mallory said.

"And the other guy?" Alex asked.

"For some reason, I had a hard time pulling an image of him off the video. I don't think he ever looks up."

Alex slowed down the clip and tried to see if she could pause it where he looked directly at the camera. But he never did. His large cowboy hat did a sufficient job of protecting his face, even when he was looking outwardly.

"Nothing," Alex said.

Instead of giving up, she scanned the images one by one, even after he left. She gasped before pumping her fist, catching Mallory's attention.

"What do you see?" Mallory asked.

"Right after the phone call, he went outside," Alex said. "Look right there in the car window. There's a reflection of him. Can you work with that?"

Mallory nodded. "I'll give it the old college try."

Alex watched anxiously as Mallory worked her magic on the computer. She enhanced and enlarged the photo before finally inserting it the facial recognition program and hitting the start key.

"Look familiar to you?" she asked.

Alex shook her head.

"Not someone else you've run into before?" Mallory asked. "A foreign agent? A terrorist operative? A former boyfriend?"

"Could be the last one," Alex said. "I definitely dated a lot of shady characters in high school."

"I'm not sure I've heard all these stories," Hawk said over the coms.

Alex laughed, forgetting that Mallory couldn't hear the other side of the conversation.

"Your response was only mildly amusing, though I don't recall you laughing so hard at your own jokes," Mallory said.

"It's something Hawk said. I'll tell you all the stories you want to know on our next vacation. Deal?"

"Deal," Hawk said. "Not that I'm jealous—just curious."

"Sure," Alex said, the sarcasm dripping from her response.

Thousands of images flickered onto the screen adjacent to the one Mallory had extracted, but nothing registered as a match. The process continued for another ten minutes with Alex and Mallory catching up on recent life events. Then the computer finally beeped, and the image next to the man from the auction house froze on the screen, ending the search.

"We have a winner," Mallory announced.

Alex leaned forward and strained to read the name in small lettering at the bottom of the photo.

"Mack Walsh," Alex read. "Ever heard of him?"

"He's a big fish," Mallory said as she opened up a search window and pecked out a web address. "Check this out."

On the monitor, the FBI's most wanted list appeared. Walsh checked in at No. 8.

"The FBI has been looking for him for over a decade," Mallory said.

CHAPTER 13

BLUNT WAS ALREADY on his second cigar by the time the team arrived at the Phoenix Foundation for an 8:00 a.m. meeting. He was anxious to learn more about the Obsidian agent as well as put together a plan to catch him. Their sole link to the organization's leadership rested in Mack Walsh, and Blunt knew they needed to find the operative or risk losing the best connection they had to Obsidian's top brass.

When the door swung open, Blunt looked up to see Alex and Hawk. Blunt leaped to his feet and motioned for them to come inside.

"Do either of you want any coffee?" Blunt asked. "I'll be more than happy to get you some."

Alex and Hawk both held up their paper mugs from a popular specialty café and declined his offer.

"You two waste so much money at that place," Blunt said. "You do realize that they over roast their beans, don't you? And that you pay more than double what you should?"

He grumbled as he meandered over to the coffee tray and poured himself another cup.

"I don't mind getting lectured," Alex said. "At least, not when it comes from someone who is a paragon of health."

"Okay, I'll leave you alone," Blunt said. "But don't come crying to me when one day you get a taste of the great stuff and wonder aloud why nobody told you about how good coffee could really be. I'm telling you right now that the mess you're drinking isn't even close to being as good as what I've brewed up here."

"You're a bit jumpy and testy this morning," Alex said. "Any reason for that?"

"Absolutely," Blunt started. "I want to learn more about this murderer, and then I want to figure out a way to get him to talk that will intimidate him into telling us all about the people running Obsidian."

"Well, I'll leave the interrogation up to Hawk and Black, but I thought you might appreciate this dossier I prepared on Mack Walsh."

"Go on," Blunt said.

Black entered the room and quickly took Blunt up on his coffee offer. Once Black settled into his seat quietly, Alex continued.

"Currently, Mack Walsh is the eighth most wanted man by the FBI for his alleged execution-style murder of a federal judge more than a decade ago," Alex said.

"A federal judge?" Blunt asked, his eyes widening. "That takes some cajones to do that."

"Yes, it does," Alex said. "But that's not all that I found interesting. Most court observers were convinced that Judge Nelson was going to rule in favor of the government on an eminent domain case. That was how Nelson had ruled more than a dozen times in the past, never once siding with the people. However, after he was murdered, the new judge reassigned to the case ruled in favor of the company, angering the government."

"Where exactly is this land?" Blunt asked.

"Idaho," she said. "Just on the edge of the Frank Church-River of No Return Wilderness Area."

"Sounds foreboding enough," Blunt said. "I'm sure you will have a wonderful time there."

"You want us to go there?" Black asked.

Blunt shrugged. "You got any better ideas?"

"I was thinking maybe we should look in Texas and see what he was up to there first," Black said. "I'd rather catch him out of his element."

"I'd rather surprise him there," Hawk said. "In my experience, people are always more relaxed in their lair. If he's out and about, he's going to be more difficult to catch."

"You two work it out," Blunt said. "I just don't want any stone unturned in our search for this guy. We need to find out more about Obsidian's plans and its hierarchy. All of our leads so far have been people co-opted into serving them. Once we can zero in on who's behind all this, maybe we can start to make some headway."

"And more importantly right now, we can avenge my mother's death," Hawk said.

Blunt threw his hands in the air. "Now, wait a minute, Hawk. I understand how you feel, but we need this guy alive."

Hawk scowled. "I'll beat all the information out of him before I end his pathetic little life."

Alex placed her hand on top of his. "Honey, it's okay. We all want this guy dead for what he did to your mother. But let's think big picture here. Your mother one day, millions of people the next. We'll make sure he gets what's coming to him."

Black nodded in agreement. "I believe it was Confucius who said, 'Before you embark on a journey of revenge, dig two graves.'"

"Well, we've already dug one," Hawk said. "And I fully intend to put that human piece of garbage in the second one."

Blunt sighed. "Just promise me that you will at least give us a chance to speak with him first."

"You have my word," Hawk said. "But then I'm going to finish him."

"Fair enough," Blunt said before standing up. "You work it out where you're going to find this punk and let me know. The jet will be fueled up and ready to take you wherever you decide."

Blunt scooped up his documents and exited the room. He knew it was going to be a furious debate, but he wanted the fledgling team to reach a consensus on its own without his involvement.

It'll be good for them.

* * *

HAWK EXHALED SLOWLY as he pondered the best way to convince Black and Alex that Idaho was a better location to hunt Hank Walsh. Looking up, Hawk scanned the ceiling as he thought.

"I'm not opposed to going to Texas," Hawk began, "but I just think our chances of catching him off guard are going to be greater in Idaho."

"We're not even sure that he's there," Black countered.

Alex's head popped up from behind her computer screen. "Yes, we do. I mean, we don't know if he's actually there now, but check this out."

She spun her screen around so they could see the pictures she'd called up.

"Before that case, here are satellite images of that plot of land the government sought to seize on the left," she said. "Now, look at this shot of the same area taken three years later. That's a big structure of some sort built right into the side of the mountain. Look at all the supporting infrastructure, too. We might have just stumbled onto Obsidian's headquarters."

"But we don't know what that place is," Black said, continuing his protest. "Walsh could've just been a hired gun to help fix a problem for whoever wanted to build that facility. If he were involved, you'd think the FBI would've captured Walsh by now."

"Maybe, maybe not," Alex said. "We already know that Obsidian has its tentacles everywhere. I wouldn't be the least bit surprised if it reached into the FBI."

Black nodded knowingly. "You make a good point, though that's sheer conjecture."

"But it's a more solid lead than trying to comb through hours of surveillance footage to find out where Walsh went after his little trip to the stockyard."

"If we go to Idaho and he's not there, that lead out of Texas is going to be worthless."

"It probably already is," Hawk said. "I'd rather smoke him out on our terms."

Black sighed. "You're like a dog with a bone on this one, Hawk."

"So, you agree we should go to Idaho?" Hawk asked.

"I'll go along with it," Black said, "but only because I know you won't change your mind any time soon. Just let it be noted that I'd prefer to go to Texas first."

"Noted," Hawk said. "Now that that's settled, let's get moving."

Black stood and collected his files. "I've always wanted to visit Idaho."

Hawk remained in his chair while Alex packed up her computer.

"Are you coming?" she asked.

"In a minute," he said. "I just need a moment alone."

She patted him on the back and leaned down to give him a kiss on the cheek.

"It's gonna be all right," she said.

"We'll catch him."

Hawk nodded knowingly and looked back down at the table, keeping his gaze there until Alex shut the door behind her. He glanced up and then pulled out his phone to text Mallory Kauffman.

I need a favor . . . and I need you to keep it between us.

CHAPTER 14

Two Days Later
River of No Return Wilderness Area
Idaho

HAWK AND THE TEAM reviewed the fine details of their plan of attack while flying from Washington to Missoula, Montana. The subsequent three-hour drive south to Salmon, Idaho was spent gawking at the rocky mountain faces and the beautiful scenery blanketing the uninhabited terrain.

"I can't believe it's taken me this long to discover Idaho," Black said.

"Idaho was discovered long ago, my friend," Hawk said. "You're just getting to enjoy it for the first time in your life."

"Well, that was far too long of a wait. Why don't more people live out here?"

"Enjoy it while it lasts," Alex said. "We'll drive right through Cobalt, Idaho, and if things pan out like investors think it will, this place might be booming in a decade from now."

"Cobalt, Idaho," Black said with a chuckle, "as in the element cobalt?"

Alex nodded. "Someone finally found a vein of cobalt in the U.S. Supposedly, it's high-level quality. So soak in this scene while it lasts."

"It'd be criminal if this all went away," Black said as he shook his head.

Hawk wheeled into the parking lot of an aging motel and checked in, securing keys for two rooms. The white paint was cracking on the slat board siding outside, while the carpet in the office had been worn thin. Hawk guessed it hadn't been changed since the mid-80s if even that soon.

In the corner, a man sporting a checkered flannel shirt with a pair of overalls rocked back and forth. He clutched a pipe in his teeth and peered over the top of his glasses at Hawk.

"What brings you to this neck of the woods?" the man said aloud.

Hawk cocked his head to one side and turned toward the old man. "What draws anyone to this part of the world? The thirst for adventure? A desire to take in the amazing beauty of these mountains?"

The old man grunted. "I find most people who come here are running."

"Running from what?"

"The past, the present. Hell, some people even run from their future. This is a great place to hide if you want to."

"We're not here to hide. I can assure you that much," Hawk said. "We're here to drink in all this place has to offer."

The old man shook his head. "What we have to offer is a great place to hide. The rest of the postcard snapshots are rare moments that we hardly ever see around here, especially in the dead of winter when Mother Nature is having her way with us. When there's ten feet of snow on the ground, you're only going to see what she wants you to see."

"I understand you're having an unseasonably warm winter this year," Hawk said.

"Yeah, only about two feet on the ground right now, but I hear a howler is coming from the west. Those are the worst. You need to watch out for them if you're going to be venturing into the wilderness area."

"We'll be careful, sir, but thanks for the heads up."

"Good luck," the old man said.

Hawk helped unload their vehicle and ushered Alex and Black to the two rooms facing Highway 93, which was heavily trafficked by tractor trailers hauling cattle, timber, and oil. Once the team settled in, they grabbed a late lunch from the only option available: a dingy diner connected to a gas station. Instead of enjoying the ambiance, they piled back into their SUV, stopping for a short spell to rent a trailer with two snowmobiles at a local outfitter company.

"Make sure you take an extra gas can with you and something to serve as a shelter in case you get stuck," the owner advised. "Snowstorms can sneak up on you out here."

Hawk nodded. "An old man at the motel we're staying at told me that a big storm was coming, but I didn't see one forecast for this area."

"That was probably Gordon Gentry. If he said there's a storm a' comin', you better believe him. He gets an ache in his knee when a blizzard is brewin'— and he's never wrong."

"I'll keep that in mind," Hawk said before they paid and left with their snow vehicles in tow.

They bumped along the U.S. Forest Service roads that had been plowed by local logging companies. Hawk rolled along, driving cautiously on the slick surface.

"Glad you got those snow tires with this SUV?" Black asked.

Hawk nodded. "We'd be walking by now if we hadn't."

He glanced up the side of the mountain,

inspecting the sparse cabins nestled up against the hillside. A few of them pumped smoke through chimneys.

"You wonder what would make a person live out in a place like this," Alex said.

"Maybe these folks just want to get away from it all—and the beach isn't their thing," Hawk said.

"Obviously, people aren't their thing either," Black said.

"There are days I wouldn't mind disappearing into the mountains never to be seen or heard from again," Hawk said. "This job will do that to you."

They continued along in silence until they reached the spot Alex had designated for them to set up their first reconnaissance mission, which was a side road that hadn't been plowed. Hawk checked his watch. It was just past 3:00 p.m.

He climbed out of the SUV, his feet sinking in the thick snow as he hit the ground. Traipsing through the powder, he walked around the front and helped Alex out. She glanced around the area, which was marked by a thick mass of tall pines and low-hanging clouds that settled over the top of the forest. A crow sat on a tree overhead and squawked at the trio of intruders.

Hawk looked skyward in the direction of the bird. "You sure you're going to be all right while we're gone?"

"I'll be monitoring you every step of the way," she said. "Besides, you know I can hold my own. I figured you'd rather have me here so I can come save you when you two get pinned down."

Black chuckled and pointed his index finger at Alex while looking at Hawk.

"She's got quite the sense of humor," Black said. "Don't let go of her."

"Maybe I don't appreciate it as much as I should since I'm usually the butt of her improv comedy routines," Hawk said.

"Yet you still have to admit that she's hilarious," Black said.

"Maybe I'll have her roast you a few times and see how you feel."

"Wait," Black said, his mouth falling agape. "The great Brady Hawk has feelings? I thought you were a tough guy. Tough guys don't have feelings."

Hawk clenched his fist and shook it at Black. "You're gonna feel this if you don't stop. We're on a reconnaissance mission, remember?"

"How could I forget," Black said as he climbed on top of a snowmobile and fired up the engine.

Hawk followed suit and backed down the ramp into the soft snow.

"Test, one, two," he said. "Test, one, two."

"I've got you loud and clear," Alex said. "I've also

got several more one-liners for both of you after you get back."

Hawk sighed as he and Black worked to unload the snowmobiles. Once they were on the ground, the two agents mounted up and rode off. After cruising along for five minutes, Alex gave them directions over the coms.

"You should see a logging road up ahead on your right," she said. "Turn there and then find a place to pull off and walk the rest of the way in. It's about a half mile directly northwest through the woods."

"Roger that," Hawk said.

Hawk and Black followed Alex's instructions, pulling their vehicles off to the side and hiding them. They put on snowshoes and slogged their way toward the property.

"Do you really expect to find Walsh here?" Black asked.

"He certainly doesn't know we're coming," Hawk said.

"At least, we think he doesn't know. There's no telling how well connected Obsidian is."

"I'm less concerned about them knowing and more worried that this could be their way to lure us in."

"If they are, we're walking in with eyes wide open," Black said.

"I prefer to storm in with guns blazing."

"I'm with you, but remember what Blunt said. We need to bring this asshole back alive."

"Yeah, I know. But that doesn't change how I feel about what I want to do to him. What would you do if you found those men who killed your father in Iraq?"

"It wouldn't be legal; I'll tell you that much. But still, we need Walsh alive."

"I heard you the first time," Hawk said.

They trudged along for ten minutes until they reached the edge of a clearing.

"You should be able to see the entrance to the property now," Alex said.

"We have visual," Hawk said.

The two agents crouched down in the snow and peered through binoculars at the side of a mountain. There was a forest service road that cut through the parcel of land and disappeared around the bend. But Hawk didn't see any signs of life or even development.

"I've got nothing," Hawk said as he continued to scan the area.

"Me either," Black said. "This looks like we were just sent on a wild goose chase."

Hawk started to get up when he froze after hearing a voice behind him.

"I strongly advise you to keep your hands where

I can see them," a man said. "And please refrain from making any quick movements."

Hawk raised his hands and slowly turned around to face an armed man in his late forties. He whistled and was joined by four other men, all with their rifles trained on the two agents.

"We're gonna need you to hand over your weapons," the man said. "And you're not gonna need those snowshoes any more either."

Hawk and Black complied, tossing their guns and shoes onto the ground near the man's feet.

"Let's go," he said. "We're gonna take a little walk."

CHAPTER 15

HAWK PLACED HIS HANDS behind his head and felt his wrists burn as one of the men cinched a tie around them. After a jarring jab in the back, Hawk stumbled forward a few feet before regaining his balance. He glanced over at Black, who was receiving the same treatment.

While Alex's silence slightly worried Hawk, he was hoping she was listening to the situation and choosing to remain silent to protect her two fellow agents. He decided to catch her up to speed through a series of questions, tipping off the men's plans as well as the location of their encampment.

"How far north are we going to walk?" Hawk asked. "Do you plan on marching us to Canada?"

"Funny guy," one of the guards said before using the butt of his rifle to whack Hawk in his ribs.

Hawk moaned as he staggered a few feet and fell down. The guard next to Hawk yanked him to his feet and shoved him forward again.

"Try to stay upright," the man grumbled. "We don't have much time."

"I didn't realize we were in a hurry," Hawk said, taking note of the tattoo on the guard's arm. Depicted were crossbones and a snake intertwined imposed over a mountain range. "Is someone going to be mad if you don't arrive on time?"

"Just shut your pie hole and keep marching," the leader said, turning around to glare at Hawk. "You'll know what you need to know when you need to know it."

Black shot Hawk a glance. "Nice try."

Hawk shrugged. "It was worth a shot."

The leader, who was referred to by his subordinates as Ringo, stopped. "What part of shut your pie hole did you not understand?"

They continued on for another ten minutes, descending into a gulch until they reached the floor. Stopping in front of what appeared to be a craggy rock face, Ringo opened a panel and entered a code. Seconds later, part of the rock swung out, revealing an entryway into the mountainside.

Hawk sighed and looked at Black.

"Maybe we need Alex to rescue us after all," Black whispered.

They moved through a couple of checkpoints until they reached a cavernous space. The rocky ceiling extended at least ten meters overhead, and the room was warmer than the chilling weather outside thanks to a system of heaters placed around the perimeter of the room. Scores of men scurried around the area, most of them armed with holstered handguns or semi-automatic weapons slung over their shoulders.

Ringo whistled and gestured for another man across the room to come over. He excused himself from a conversation and hustled over.

"What's going on? Who are these guys?" the man asked.

"Caught them snooping around in the woods, Chief," Ringo said. "They look like feds."

Chief stroked his scraggly, graying beard as he eyed Hawk and Black closely. "You sure they're feds?"

"I didn't ask them," Ringo said. "But look at their weapons. They certainly weren't out hunting game with those guns."

Chief used his fist to lift up Hawk's chin. "Are you a fed?"

Hawk shook his head. "No, sir."

Chief shrugged and looked at Ringo. "See, all you had to do was ask. Now you've made a mess out of things since you brought them back here."

"Brought us back where?" Hawk asked. "I don't know where I am, nor do I care."

Chief chuckled and pointed at Hawk. "I like this guy already."

Everyone nearby broke into laughter before Chief darted behind Hawk and put a knife to his throat.

"I'm only gonna ask you one more time, and this time I want the truth," Chief said. "Are you two feds?"

"Former Navy SEAL," Hawk said. "My friend is a mercenary for hire. We're not looking for you."

"Just who are you looking for?"

"In my back pocket is a photo of the guy," Hawk said. "Mack Walsh. Ever heard of heard of him?"

Chief pulled out the picture and studied it for a moment. "Never heard of a Mack Walsh, but I know this guy. His name is Billy Youngblood."

"You bounty hunters?" Ringo asked.

Hawk nodded. "More or less. I promise you that we're not here to make any trouble with you and whatever this is."

Chief nodded at one of his underlings, the gesture understood. A knife ripped through the bindings, releasing Hawk and Black. They both rubbed their wrists and thanked the man for cutting them loose.

"So, can you help us find him?" Hawk asked.

"Normally, we keep to ourselves around here and wouldn't rat any locals out, no matter what they were doing," Chief said. "But Billy Youngblood isn't from around here. I wouldn't mind seeing less of him in these parts."

"He has a mountain?" Black asked.

"That's how we refer to it, but some corporation somewhere bought it years ago. Youngblood just manages it, so to speak. He oversaw all the construction there five or six years ago. Beyond that, I don't really know much. People don't take too kindly to others sticking their noses where they don't belong. We just leave each other alone, and we all get along just fine."

"But Youngblood is different?" Hawk asked.

Chief shrugged. "He's just not one of us, and I have no idea what he's really about. However, if you're looking for him, it appears he's up to no good."

"You could say that," Hawk said.

"Ringo, give these gentlemen their weapons back," Chief said. "We don't want any trouble around here, especially with no bounty hunters."

"But, Chief," Ringo protested, "they've been to our lair now and they could—"

"It's all your fault anyway, but I don't think they're going to report us to anybody, now are you?"

Hawk shook his head. "Report what to who?"

Chief laughed. "These guys get it. We don't need to trouble them any longer. Ringo, why don't you escort them out?"

Black held up his index finger. "Before we go, you mentioned that Youngblood oversaw some construction on his mountain. You got any idea what he was building?"

"Not really," Chief said. "Just lots of big trucks streaming materials in and out every day for about six months. The place is guarded like a fortress now, though I'm not sure anybody's ever come around looking for it—until now."

"A fortress?" Hawk asked.

"You best be careful around there," Chief said. "I'd keep a safe distance if I were you and stay on this side of the river. I doubt you'd get the same kind of reception you got here. In fact, I'd guarantee it."

CHAPTER 16

A GUARD ESCORTED HAWK and Black outside to the perimeter of the property and handed them their snowshoes. He nodded at them before turning and walking away. The two operatives strapped on their shoes, and Hawk hailed Alex on his coms.

"That was close," she said. "What the hell was that?"

"As far as I can tell, they were some militia group," Hawk said.

"They let you off easily from what I could hear."

"I'd say we were fortunate," Hawk said. "Apparently, they aren't very fond of Mack Walsh—or Billy Youngblood, as they known him."

"But the good news is we now know exactly where he is and how to get there," Black said. "And we also know that this isn't some ragtag outpost either."

"Oh?" Alex said. "That must've been the part where I couldn't hear much of what was going on."

"Yeah," Black continued, "there was some major construction happening that nobody around here knows much about."

"We've got a lot to discuss then," she said. "Get back here as soon as possible, and let's regroup for tomorrow. You don't have much daylight left."

* * *

THE NEXT MORNING, the team returned to the area, this time parking much closer to the edge of Walsh's property. After considering all the intel gleaned from the militia group, the team decided to deploy a drone to get a closer look.

"It won't be long before we're all replaced by drones," Hawk said as he huddled over Alex's left shoulder to get a look at the image transmitted back to her computer.

Black, who was standing to Alex's right, flexed his bicep. "They'll never be able to replace these."

Alex shot him a sideways glance. "Wanna bet? If there are combat ready drones, I can guarantee you they won't charge in when they shouldn't."

"That hurts, Alex. I thought all was forgiven."

"Forgiven, but not forgotten," she said with a wink.

The drone wove through the forest, hovering smoothly above the snow-coated vegetation. After a couple minutes, the device entered an area far less dense with charred pine remnant emerging from the ground like spikes.

"What happened here?" Alex wondered aloud.

"It looks like there was a fire at some point," Hawk said.

Alex pointed at the screen and rotated the camera. "Look at this though. It's almost a perfect circle, like it was a controlled burn."

"Or an explosion," Black said.

"Freaky," Alex said before navigating the drone out of the area.

A couple minutes later, the drone wound along the river and came within several hundred meters of where Chief had said the edge of Walsh's property was. Then the camera started to flash in and out.

"What's going on?" Hawk asked.

Alex scowled as she hammered away on her keyboard. "I'm not sure. Everything is functioning correctly as far as I can tell."

"Well, something's not right," Hawk said.

"We're getting some kind of interference," she said. "It's like there's an electromagnetic field that's disrupting everything."

A few seconds later, the camera blinked and then went completely black.

"We lost the signal," Alex said.

"Well, we need to get closer than that," Hawk said.

"And we can't leave a drone lying just outside the entrance to the hideout," Black added. "If they find it, we'll lose the element of surprise."

"If we still have it," Alex said. "How do you know that those militiamen weren't playing you yesterday?"

"We don't," Hawk said, "but when I looked at Chief's face when he was talking about the man he knows as Billy Youngblood, the contempt was genuine. You just can't fake that."

"In that case, you boys better suit up," she said. "The mountain awaits you."

* * *

HAWK AFFIXED A BODY CAM to the strap on his pack and turned the device on before heading out with Black.

"Can you hear me?" Hawk asked over his coms.

"Loud and clear," Alex said.

"Good. We're going to get your drone back and figure out what's going on here."

"I don't like it, Hawk."

"I know," he said. "I can tell you're apprehensive about this mission. What's going on?"

"I don't know. I just can't shake this bad feeling I have. These people we're dealing with, they're—" She stopped abruptly, suspending her thought.

"They're what?" Hawk asked. "Is everything all right?"

"Yeah," she said slowly, "everything is fine. I just got chills thinking about what might happen if we don't stop these people."

"We'll stop them. Don't worry," Hawk said as he turned and looked at Black. "You've got two of the best agents on the case."

Black chuckled. "You've got the second best agent and me. You're in luck."

"You better be as good as advertised," Alex said. "This is your chance to prove it."

Hawk and Black moved along the same path as the drone, reaching the charred area and forging ahead without taking too much time to examine it. Black surveyed the damage and nodded.

"This was definitely an explosion," he said. "No doubt about it."

A few minutes later, they arrived at the spot where the drone started to go on the blink.

"There's the drone," Hawk said.

Alex gave a celebratory whoop. "Hopefully it's not fried."

"I'll let you be the judge of that," Hawk said as he knelt down and picked it up. "Are you getting this?"

No reply.

"Alex, are you there?"

Nothing—except a screeching noise in his ear from the coms. He backed up a few meters before speaking again.

"Alex?" he tried again. "Are you there?"

"Oh, there you are," she said. "You went out for a moment, just like the drone."

"Well, I can't see much of anything new from here," he said. "But there's definitely something inside that mountain. And we're going to need to get a little closer to check it out some more."

"I don't think that's a good idea," Alex said.

"Why's that?"

"You're about three miles away from here, and it just started snowing like crazy."

"The old man was right," Hawk said with a chuckle.

"What old man?"

"Never mind. I'll explain later."

"So are you coming back now?" she asked. "I might be covered up by the time you get here if you don't hurry."

Hawk sighed. "This is our chance to find out what this place is. We haven't seen a single guard from here, and if we're going to break inside, we at least need to know what we're up against."

"I don't like this, Hawk."

"We'll make it quick. I promise."

Hawk nodded at Black before they moved forward and crossed the small tributary that wasn't much more than a trickle. After hopping over it, Hawk looked up and noticed a large pole poorly disguised as a tree with several communication dishes attached near the top.

"Think that's where the magnetic field is being generated?" Hawk asked.

Black stopped and stared up. "That's what I'd put my money on. I see some devices pointed toward the ground and several aimed skyward."

"All right. Let's keep moving. Just remember that."

After they plodded along for a few more minutes in silence, Black started a conversation.

"You know, charging ahead without going back and forth about it is so much easier," Black said.

"You'd like that, wouldn't you?" Hawk asked.

Black nodded.

"Yeah, well, we're a team and we work together like one," Hawk said. "You don't just race into a potentially dangerous situation without discussing it first."

"I'm here, aren't I?"

Hawk shook his head. "You've got some nerve. I'll tell you that much. I suppose you forgot that we're down one less terrorist in custody because of your stunt in Sudan."

"I got quite a bit of intel on Evana Bahar and how Al Fatihin operates."

"That information is probably worthless by now as much as they move around. We speculated that Evana was making a move to retrieve Ramin Torabi so she could ingratiate herself to his father, Amir, who also is the head of HadithTel and could fund Al Fatihin for years. And if that's the case, I think you know who got the short end of that trade."

"Not if I'm the one who brings them down."

"We will bring them down," Hawk said. "But how many more innocent people might die before we do?"

Black remained silent as they forged through the forest and made their way closer to Walsh's property boundary. Hawk noticed a guard patrolling the area a few meters away and scrambled to the ground, dragging Black down as well.

Hawk rolled into a prone position and looked at Black, who had pulled out his binoculars and was scanning the surrounding area.

"How many men do you see?" Hawk asked in a whisper.

Black held up his hand. "Five," he said. "All armed. And these don't look like stiffs with a weapon either."

"So, we're in for a fight?"

"If we try this now—and who knows how many more are behind that door."

"Door?" Hawk asked. "What door?"

A large section of the rock against the side of the mountain began to slide upward.

"Would you look at that," Black said. "Those militiamen weren't kidding when they said some major construction was going on here. What is Obsidian hiding inside there?"

"What else do you see?"

"Looks like there's a checkpoint of some kind and definitely more men inside. Oh, and there he is, Mr. Walsh himself."

Hawk snatched the binoculars from Black without a word and surveyed the scene.

"I think I could take him out right now," Hawk said.

"Look who's acting impulsively now," Black said. "We need to bring him back alive, remember?"

"Forget that. I want that asshole dead."

"We both do, but we need to think this through. We need to get a plan together and come back here and light these guys up—and bring Walsh back alive."

The snow started to come down harder as the wind picked up. With the flakes falling thick, Hawk's visibility was reduced to little more than a hundred meters. He heard what sounded like a truck revving up its engine before a snowplow emerged from the entrance and started clearing a pathway.

Hawk waited until the guard that was nearby retreated inside before standing up.

"Let's go," Hawk said. "Tomorrow, we're gonna burn this place to the ground."

CHAPTER 17

AFTER DIGGING OUT their truck from the foot of snow that fell during the hour it took Black and Hawk to meet back up with Alex, they returned to their motel. Outside, the wind howled against their door, which allowed a frigid draft inside. Meanwhile, the snow continued to fall heavily.

After grabbing some sandwiches from a sub shop next door, they retreated to their room to plot out their mission assignments for the next day. But Hawk seemed resistant to any idea that didn't end with him shooting Walsh. All Hawk wanted was revenge.

"The mission is to bring Walsh back alive," Black said.

"You're the one who penetrated Obsidian," Hawk said. "Why can't you do it again? And maybe this time, you can find out more about them than just who their co-opted foot soldiers are."

"It doesn't work like that," Black said. "I'm familiar with how they operate, but it's the who that we don't know. Walsh is obviously over the operation here and would be a big get for us."

"I doubt he knows much of anything. And we're out here wasting our time on trying to catch him."

"I get it, Hawk. You're angry—and rightly so—over what he did to your mother. But this is the closest we've gotten to anyone other than Obsidian's extensive network of underlings who are executing the group's plans on the ground. If we're going to stop them from murdering other innocent mothers and fathers and children, you need to set aside your vendetta. Walsh was obviously giving orders to Dr. Becker, and if Walsh can lead us one level higher, that'll put us one step closer to shutting down Obsidian."

Hawk sighed and paced around the room. Alex stepped into his path and eyed him carefully, forcing him to stop.

"It's all right to be angry," Alex said. "I think we all want the son of a bitch dead eventually. He needs to answer for what he did. But you of all people understand the importance of unraveling a terrorist cell from the inside out. You can't expect to make any headway by avenging every terrible act they commit. We want the head of the snake, and right now, Walsh is the link we need to get us that."

Hawk looked down and remained quiet. He

knew she was right about everything as usual. Yet he couldn't help but feel rage burning within him every time Walsh's name was mentioned. For the past six months, each night when Hawk put his head on his pillow, he imagined a final confrontation with his mother's killer and the conversation that would take place. Hawk rehearsed his lines and knew precisely what he would say before emptying every bullet he had into the man's chest and head. Coming to grips with the fact that Hawk's vengeful fantasy needed to be scuttled for the sake of the overall mission was challenging to accept.

"Are you all right?" Alex asked, breaking the silence.

Hawk shook his head. "I won't be all right until Walsh has paid for what he did."

"I understand, but can you wait until we've got everything we need from him to drill deeper into Obsidian?"

Hawk nodded confidently. "For the sake of the mission, I think I can."

"Good," she said, placing her hands on his biceps and looking him directly in the eyes. "We need to be able to count on you and know that you're not going to do something that would jeopardize the mission."

"I won't let this team down," he said.

"There's my Hawk," she said as a faint smile crept across her lips. "Now, let's get to work planning on how we're going to conquer this mountain."

* * *

THE NEXT MORNING, the team slowly made its way along the roads blanketed with yet another fresh coat of snow. Plows had been cruising along Highway 93 all night long to keep the paved roads as clean as possible, but the U.S. Forest Service roads proved to be somewhat challenging. The storm had blown through, but thick gray clouds still hung overhead.

As the team bumped along, they all craned their necks when the thumping beat of a helicopter blade interrupted the otherwise quiet drive.

"What do you think that's all about?" Alex asked.

"Your guess is as good as mine," Hawk said. "But I can only imagine that it's related to Obsidian. If we're lucky, it'll be a high-ranking official making his way to inspect whatever it is that's going on here."

Struggling to keep their SUV moving straight due to the slick surface, Hawk worked hard not to spill his coffee. The rigorous hike the day before resulted in a solid night of sleep, but the fatigue from the physical demand as well as the emotional nature of the mission was starting to take a toll on him. He was hoping the caffeine would kick in soon.

While they rode, they discussed the obstacles

posed by the new snow. Hawk and Black decided that they would have to take snowmobiles to reduce their time reaching the entrance of the Obsidian facility. Alex would be left alone to fend for herself while tracking their progress from her computer terminal.

"I'm not going to be much help once you reach the gate," she said. "If that magnetic field that caused all those problems yesterday is still up and running, you're flying blind without me."

"And if we turn it off?" Black asked.

"That'd be great, but I wouldn't make that a priority," she said. "The objective is to apprehend Walsh."

Hawk nodded. "We'll do our best to get that field down. It'd be helpful to have you watching our backs."

"I'm not sure how much good I'll be able to do, especially if either one of you decides to charge into danger again."

"I'll be good," Black said. "I promise."

"Hawk?"

"You know me."

"I know," she said. "That's why I'm wondering if you're going to heed my warning. We don't need to go over this again, do we?"

Hawk shook his head. "I'm focused and don't need to be reminded about what's at stake here."

"That's what I like to hear. Now, let's go get Mack Walsh."

Hawk and Black struck out toward the Obsidian facility, slogging their way through the fresh snow. Even with the proper equipment, their speed was hampered.

Once they neared the spot where the magnetic field interfered with their communications, Hawk warned Alex that they might be losing contact.

"Roger that," she said.

Hawk scaled the tower poorly disguised as a tree, ascending via the ladder welded to the side. Once he reached the top, he jimmied open an electrical box and cut a few wires before attempting to hail Alex.

"Can you hear me?" he asked.

Nothing.

He went back to work, yanking out some wires and slashing others. Then he tried again.

"Alex, can you hear me?"

More silence.

Without any other options to disrupt the field, Hawk scurried down the ladder to move away from the boundary to discuss the situation with Alex and Black.

"Could you hear me at all a few minutes ago?" Hawk asked.

"I just heard some static," she said. "Did you disable the field?"

Hawk shrugged. "I thought so, but maybe that

isn't the source of the magnetism. Maybe there's something else."

"It's probably coming from inside that mountain," Black said.

"Think they have some kind of reactor in there?" Alex asked.

"We haven't gotten close enough to see inside yet," Hawk said. "But we're going to do our best."

Black looked over Hawk's shoulder and pointed. "We've gotta move."

Hawk turned and noticed several guards filing out of a hidden door beside the main entrance. "We've got company headed this way."

Then a large truck rumbled down the plowed road leading to the main checkpoint.

"That's our way in," Hawk said.

Black nodded. "Agreed. Let's go."

"Alex, we need to go. This is a gift of a chance to gain access to the facility and find out what's going on."

"Hawk! You're not supposed to be making impulsive decisions here. We need to get inside, but both of you can't be put at risk."

"Why not?" Black said. "You're going to come save us if we're captured, aren't you?"

"That's not funny, you two. I'm telling you right now that this is a bad idea. Stay where you are, and don't make any rash decisions."

"I'm sorry," Hawk said. "You're breaking . . . up . . . on . . . us."

He nodded at Black, and they both raced for the road.

"She's gonna kill us, man," Black said.

"Not if we don't get caught," Hawk replied.

They scrambled up a small ridge and unhitched their snowshoes before darting right behind the slow-moving transport truck, which was inching its way toward the gate. Hawk and Black both grabbed onto the back, using the bumper for a foothold while clinging to the tailgate. The bed was exposed and packed full of wooden crates.

"You ready to do this?" Hawk asked.

Black nodded. "You?"

"This is my favorite part of the job."

"Mine too. Let's stick tight until we can get a lay of the land."

"Roger that," Hawk said.

The truck's brake lights flashed as the vehicle came to a stop. Hawk and Black scrambled underneath and used their belts to stay suspended above the ground by wrapping them around the axel.

Hawk looked down at the ground around the driver's side of the truck. A pair of boots crunched in the scant amount of snow that had survived a recent plowing.

"You have any trouble getting in here?" a guard asked the driver.

"Smooth sailing, all things considered."

"All right. Well, just sit tight while we make sure you don't have any hitchhikers aboard."

"Take your time. I've got nowhere else to be today."

Hawk felt his hand slipping as he and Black both rolled onto the top of the axel. After repositioning, Hawk steadied himself and took a deep breath before slowly exhaling. He and Black stayed frozen while the guard did a cursory check. He gave a half-hearted attempt to see anything beneath the truck's carriage but cleared it after less than a half-minute of searching.

Hawk thought they were in the clear as the guard approached the driver's side door again. But then he stopped and whistled.

"Bring out the lads," the guard said.

Hawk swallowed hard as the sound of dogs barking echoed off the mountainside. Seconds later, they were sniffing all around the bottom of the truck. Hawk glanced down and looked eye-to-eye at one of the German Shepherds. It growled at Hawk.

"Whoa, girl," one of the guards said as he yanked on the dog's leash. "You're mighty testy this morning. You see something under there?"

The dog barked several times, straining to escape its master's grasp.

"All right. Settle down. I'll have a look," the guard said.

Hawk tightened his grip with his left hand before reaching for his gun. He slowly removed it from the holster and clicked off the safety.

CHAPTER 18

HAWK DIDN'T FLINCH as the guard fell to his knees in the snow. He let out a few expletives after he set down his coffee and it spilled when the German Shepherd's wagging tail smacked the cup. The dog barked some more and tried to resist the harness, keeping him from returning beneath the truck.

"Damn it, Brutus," the guard said. "You're always making a mess of things. Hal, can you hold this stupid mutt for me? There's either twenty-five armed men under the carriage or a whole barrel of bacon."

"Sure thing, Doug. I'm hoping she smells bacon."

Doug chuckled. "You and me both."

Hawk watched as the guard stood upright and walked around to the other side of the truck. "Did you fellas check underneath here first?"

"Yeah," came the reply. "I didn't see anything."

"Okay, well, Brutus is about to have a coronary over there. I just wanted to make sure you did your due diligence."

"Nothing in there, sir."

"I hope you're right," Doug said. "I'm going to check once more."

A few seconds later, Hawk noticed a mirror attached to a black stick eased beneath the edge of the vehicle. He couldn't see the face of the man operating the device, though he was sure it was Doug based on the man's shoes. And the fact that Hawk couldn't see his face was a good thing, meaning the mirror wasn't positioned at the correct angle.

"I haven't had to use this damn thing very much," Doug said. "The mirror keeps slipping down."

"I just say the hell with it and let the truck pass," another guard suggested.

"Nope, gotta do this right," Doug said. He pulled the stick back before reinserting it. This time, the mirror detached completely and fell off the rod before shattering on top of a large rock.

"Not again," Doug moaned. He fell to his knees and grabbed the broken mirror without glancing upward.

"I'm done with this," he said. "Let's just let Brutus run around extra today to get some of that energy out. I'm sure it's nothing."

"All right, move along," one of the other guards said.

The truck clicked into gear and rolled forward

slowly into the mountain. Hawk was surprised at their good fortune, but it was cold and they likely had never had anyone attempt to infiltrate their fortress of a facility.

"Am I the last one?" the driver asked.

"Everything else went out last week," another man said. "According to my supervisor, production is almost complete, and they'll have everything they need by this afternoon."

"Great," the driver said. "I'm tired of making this drive every week. Got any idea where they're moving to?"

"They don't tell me stuff like that. I just keep my head down and do what I'm told."

The driver hopped out of the truck and slammed the door before walking off with the other man. Hawk eased himself onto the ground along with Black.

"What is this place?" Black asked in a whisper.

"Let's find out," Hawk said.

He noticed most of the employees wore bright-orange vests and hard hats. On a nearby wall, a row of hooks held both items.

"Follow me," Hawk said.

Hawk and Black rolled out from underneath the truck and scrambled to their feet before hustling over to the wall to get into the facility's proper attire. Once outfitted, Hawk scanned the area before suggesting

176 | R.J. PATTERSON

their next move.

The cavernous operation consisted of a half dozen steel vats that towered two stories high. Workers scurried up and down the steps and appeared to be checking valve readouts of some sort. Surrounding the open space were offices and labs.

"The U.N. was a trial run," Hawk said. "They're still producing a virus here."

"Or an antidote," Black offered.

"Either way, if this is what's been going on, we've missed it—and it's been right under our noses."

"And they're about to leave this place," Black said. "Probably with everything they need."

"We're just looking for Walsh, remember?"

Black huffed a laugh through his nose. "That was before we laid eyes on all this. We need to end this now."

"We need to complete the mission, which is apprehending Walsh."

"Don't tell me you would shed a tear if he went up in smoke along with the rest of this plant."

Hawk shrugged. "Probably not. But Alex is right. I can't let my personal vendetta get in the way. When we get out of here, if we don't have Walsh, we've failed."

"I guess that depends on how you look at things," Black said. "Delaying Obsidian's production schedule and incinerating this place before they're through isn't exactly a failure in my book. We're supposed to be keeping America safe, aren't we?"

Hawk glared at Black. "Stick to the plan, okay?"

"The plan needs to change, and I think you know that."

"I'm not gonna fight you on this," Hawk said.

"Good because you'd lose anyway."

Before Hawk could respond, Black darted up a set of nearby stairs and made his way to the second floor. Hawk raced after his partner, catching him on the landing.

"What are you doing?" Hawk asked.

"I'm about to get this party started," Black said.

"What about Walsh?"

"Have you seen him?"

"I've hardly had a chance to look."

Black scanned the area below, keeping his weapon holstered. "With or without Walsh, this place needs to go up in smoke. You've got five minutes, and then it's Operation Armageddon."

"Come on, man. Give me more time than that. Besides, you can't sabotage this place that quickly."

"Bet me," Black said before he paused to gaze across the production floor. "Okay, you've got ten minutes and then I'm going to light this place up."

"Ten minutes and not a second earlier," Hawk said.

Black nodded and followed Hawk down the steps. He watched as his partner dashed off toward a large tank of fuel, where one worker stood with a dispenser in his hand as he pumped gas into a truck.

"We're all dead," Hawk mumbled to himself.

He changed his focus toward the rooms encircling the main production area. The most challenging part was discerning which rooms were offices and which were labs. They all seemed roughly the same size, but he quickly noted that the offices were smaller and tighter spaces, while the labs extended deep into the exterior.

Hawk hustled down the steps and began a more in-depth reconnaissance mission, noting which rooms were reserved for management and which ones were designated for Obsidian scientists. While he was casually breezing past several of the rooms, he stopped and froze.

Dr. Becker was inside one of the labs.

Hawk spun around and hustled back to the floor where Black was working to sabotage the vats.

"This just got really tricky," Hawk said.

"What is it?" Black said, continuing to leak fuel at the bottom of the steel structures.

"Becker's here."

"What?"

"Yeah, he's in a lab upstairs and looks like he's

about to test some patients."

Black sighed. "You want to bring him back along with Walsh—that is if we can find him?"

"That's what I'm thinking."

"Corralling both of them will be tricky considering what kind of hellfire we're about to unleash on this place."

"I don't care," Hawk said. "He'll have some answers for us."

"Okay, we'll make it work. I'll give you five minutes to convince Becker to go along with you. Then I'm going to light this place up. Hopefully, the explosion will flush out Walsh if he's here and I'll take him down. If we get separated, let's meet back at the site where we breached the perimeter next to the communications tower."

"Alex is gonna kill us," Hawk said.

"Or rescue us," Black said with a wry grin. "We haven't escaped this place yet."

Hawk nodded. "Five minutes."

"Go."

Hawk raced up the steps to the second level and returned to the lab where he'd seen Becker. The doctor was preparing some sort of mixture to inject in the patients with an assistant. Against the far wall, five patients sat blindfolded, apparently unwilling to be tested.

Hawk entered the room and locked it behind him.

"Can I help you?" Becker said without looking.

Hawk clicked the safety off his weapon and trained it on Becker. "Doc, I need you to come with me."

Becker stopped and looked up at Hawk. "What do you think you're doing?"

"I'm saving these people," Hawk said. "And I'm taking you hostage."

The patients started to murmur amongst themselves.

"What's going on?" one of them asked. A man on the far end of the row removed his blindfold.

"I warned you there would be consequences if you took off your mask," the assistant said as he drew his weapon. He did hesitate to pull the trigger, hitting the patient in the head. The man crumpled to the ground.

"Anyone else have questions?" the assistant asked.

Hawk wheeled around and put two bullets in the assistant, one in his chest and the other in his head.

Becker shook his head and stamped his foot. "I thought you were one of the good guys."

"I am," Hawk said. "That's why I just shot and killed your murdering assistant."

Becker picked up his syringe and squeezed it slightly as he watched the liquid drip from the point.

"I'm about to save these people's lives," Becker said. "And they don't even know it yet."

"No," Hawk said as he retrained his gun on Becker. "You're going to let these people go and come with me."

Becker rolled his eyes. "I don't think so." He marched over to the patient next to the dead man slumped on the floor and searched for a vein.

"If you value you your own life, you'll drop that syringe," Hawk said.

"If you valued yours, you'd let me inject you with this," Becker fired back. "You just don't get it, do you? I'm the one who's going to save all these people, not you."

"I'm not going to warn you again," Hawk said as he moved closer to Becker. "Drop it."

Becker glanced back at Hawk. "What are you going to do? Shoot me?"

"If I have to, yes."

"I thought you were nobler than to shoot an unarmed man."

"Nobility has nothing to do with it. If you want to keep testing my limits, just make another move."

Becker ignored Hawk and tapped the forearm of the patient in search of a vein. Hawk fired his gun, sending the patients into a further panic.

"I'm not doing this anymore," one of the women said before ripping off her mask and lunging toward the door.

Becker reached up and grabbed her, flinging her against her chair. "You're not going anywhere."

"Yes, she is," Hawk said as he jammed his gun into Becker's back. "In fact, you're all free to go. And I encourage you to run as far as you can away from this place."

The remaining masked patients almost in unison removed their blindfolds and dashed toward the exit, leaving Hawk alone with Becker. Once the door latched shut, Hawk turned his gaze toward Becker.

"You can't say that I didn't warn you," Hawk said.

"Feel free to warn me all you like, but you are in way over your head here," Becker said. "If anyone is going to survive the virus that's about to be unleashed on this planet, it's going to be because of the brave men and women who donate their bodies to science."

"How many have survived?" Hawk asked.

"That's the beside the point."

"No, that's exactly the point. If people aren't surviving, you are failing. And nothing Obsidian wants to do is going to work without making sure that they have an antidote to extort nations and their key influencers to do what's necessary to help this organization take control."

"That's right. And I figured it was better to get on board now before it was too late," Becker said as he grabbed his shoulder.

"Getting shot is painful," Hawk said. "But I don't need to tell you that."

"No, you don't."

"Then drop the syringe and come with me. We can help put an end to these ridiculous notions of Obsidian."

"They're more powerful than you can even imagine," Becker said. "I heard they even got to your mother, who was under federal protection."

Hawk glared at Becker. "Watch it."

"I'm not as evil as you think, Mr. Hawk. We're on the same side, you know."

"And what side is that?"

"The side of humanity."

Hawk huffed. "If you cared about humanity, you wouldn't be doing what you're doing."

"And what do you think I'm doing? Killing patients for sport?"

"You're certainly not healing anyone."

"That's where you're wrong," Becker said. "We've had several cases where people have recovered thanks to the antidote I'm studying."

"Several cases out of how many trial subjects?

Hundreds? Thousands? Millions?"

"Don't be absurd. Nothing would ever get that far without drawing attention from watchdog groups. No, what we're doing is so special and so secretive that nobody even knows about it."

"And you trust the patients who just sprinted out of this room to get away from you?"

"They're being monitored," Becker said. "Any sudden change in pulse and we can activate something we planted inside of them, killing them instantly. It'll look like a heart attack to everyone investigating the death, but I will know the truth—and so do you now."

"Why tell me all this?" Hawk said. "You're certainly not endearing yourself to me by pulling back the curtain on your operation."

"You won't make it out alive," Becker said. "That much I know. I figured you ought to know before you die."

"Doc, I'm the one holding the gun here."

"But I'm the one holding the syringe," Becker said.

With that, Becker injected himself in the arm.

"What are you doing?" Hawk asked.

"Saving the world," Becker snapped. "Just you watch."

Before either of them could move, an explosion rocked the area downstairs. Hawk rushed over to the window and watched as the production portion of the hideout began to explode.

Hawk couldn't do anything but watch as Becker jammed the need into his arm, convulsed, and then shake back and forth on his own. The seizure overtook his entire body. He thrashed all around before falling to the ground in a heap of exhaustion.

"Okay, that's enough theatrics," Hawk said as he looked at Becker, who had progressed to writhing on the floor.

Becker spewed bile out of his mouth. He was still alive but barely hanging on.

Hawk cursed as he rushed over to check on Becker. There was a pulse, but not much of one.

"Damn it," Hawk said as he started to pace around the room. "What a fool."

The fire outside the door started to rage. Hawk turned and looked at Becker, who was moving toward his dead assistant.

"He can't help you now," Hawk said. "He's dead."

Becker ignored Hawk and kept inching his way toward the assistant spotting the gun. Without hesitating, Becker picked it up and placed the barrel underneath his chin.

"Don't do it," Hawk screamed.

"The pain," Becker stammered. "I'm dead

anyway."

Becker squeezed the trigger. His body fell limp as he crashed to the floor.

Hawk rushed over to the window as large chunks of the ceiling started to plummet downward. The ground shook as more explosions rocked the mountain. He ran outside, grabbing onto the railing to maintain his balance as he searched for Black.

After a brief scan of the space below, Hawk didn't see his partner. However, Hawk noticed Mack Walsh.

Stay calm, Hawk.

Hawk's adrenalin surged, blood rushing to his head as he unleashed a primal scream. He hustled down the stairs and sprinted straight for Walsh. When the two men collided, Hawk sent Walsh flying against the wall. Hawk stumbled but managed to maintain his balance, while Walsh grimaced and shook his head.

"You're coming with me, you son of a bitch," Hawk said with a growl.

Walsh narrowed his eyes and glared at Hawk.

"Don't try anything," Hawk warned. "I won't hesitate to take you out right here."

Another explosion drew their attention away from the conversation as they both watched another vat become engulfed in flames. Hawk was about to make his final appeal to Walsh when Black rushed over to the scene.

"We gotta get out of here, Hawk."

"Already? I just found Walsh."

Black looked around. "Where?"

Hawk turned his focus toward the spot where Walsh had just been. "He was right there."

"In about thirty seconds, it won't matter who we've got because we'll both be dead if we don't hurry," Black said. "Come with me."

Black ran in the opposite direction of the entrance, instead sprinting away from it.

"What are we doing?" Hawk said. "The gate is that way."

"Just shut up and run," Black said. "Trust me."

A few seconds later, Black flung open a door and barely stopped his momentum in time to avoid plunging headlong off a cliff. Hawk poked his head out and saw that they were standing on a rock that jutted out over a snow-covered ravine. By his best estimate, Hawk figured they were about twenty meters off the ground.

"What do you want to do now?" he asked.

"Jump," Black said. "It's our only option."

"I don't think so," Hawk said. "We have no idea what's underneath all this snow."

"It's either that or get consumed in the fire."

Hawk eyed the craggy rock face nearby to see if

he could climb it or maneuver around another way to safety.

"This mountain is going to explode in about ten seconds. We don't have time to plot our way down. We just have to jump."

"I know you're not serious," Hawk said. "We should just—"

An explosion rattled the floor as it started to split beneath them. Then Black lunged forward, wrapping his arms around Hawk before the two tumbled off the ledge and plummeted toward the snow below.

CHAPTER 19

HAWK BRACED FOR IMPACT, covering his head and hoping that if he died, his death would be a quick one. He looked at Black, whose eyes were wild with delight. He seemed to enjoy flirting with death.

"Here goes nothing," Black said with a wink.

Black released his hold on Hawk as the two crashed into the snow. Once Hawk regained his bearings, he could tell he fell feet first and only needed to climb up a few feet to reach the surface.

"Black? You there?"

"Alive and kickin'," Black answered. "But we can't afford to stay here for long."

"Why's that?"

"Look at the mountainside. These are prime conditions for an avalanche. Fresh loose snow, warming weather, and a seismic event."

"What's happening out there?" Hawk asked as he worked his way up and out of the snow.

"That explosion is acting like a seismic event. It

can easily shake loose an avalanche."

A few seconds later, Hawk reached the surface first. He took a deep breath, inhaling a lungful of mountain air tinged with smoke. Black's head popped up out of the snow next.

"Ready to run?" Black asked as he wriggled out of the shallow cave he made for himself when he fell.

"I had Walsh," Hawk said. "But you screwed it all up when you came over."

"If I hadn't interfered, you wouldn't have him now anyway," Black said. "You'd be dead right along with him."

"Until I see his cold dead body, I'm not so sure I'll believe that he's dead."

"Don't be so stubborn," Black said. "It's highly improbable he could've survived that explosion. Speaking of which, we need to move."

Hawk stood and started to follow Black through the snow.

"Pick it up," Black said.

Hawk started to run but stopped suddenly when he heard Alex's voice crackling over his earpiece.

"Hawk? Black?" she called. "Can either of you hear me?"

"Loud and clear, honey," Hawk said.

"It's so good to hear your voice," she said.

"We're both fine, but I'm afraid we can't chit chat

right now," Black said. "We're in a bit of a jam. An avalanche is shaking loose, and we're going to be right in its path if we don't get to safety quickly."

"Roger that," Alex said. "You didn't happen to get Walsh, did you?"

Hawk was about to tell her the story while he ran, but he lost his balance when sheets of snow barreled just along the surface in his direction. His legs flew out from beneath him as he started to bounce along on his butt. Unable to change course or slow himself down, Hawk was at the mercy of Mother Nature.

The snow whisked him down the slope at an increasing speed. He managed to avoid trees on his left and right, sliding just beneath some branches. After waiting a moment, he stopped and slowly stood to celebrate his survival.

Hawk looked over at Black, who was waving his arms wildly.

"Behind you," Black said. "Run!"

Hawk glanced over his shoulder to see a wave of snow rolling down the hill. He followed Black's lead and tried to sprint through the snow. However, Hawk looked more like he was slogging through a swamp as the snow was waist deep.

"You need to jump as high as you can just before the snow reaches you," Black said. "And hold one hand up in the air. It's coming in three, two, one . . ."

Hawk didn't even look, trusting his colleague running parallel fifty meters to the left. As Black counted down, Hawk positioned his feet as close to the surface as he could and mustered all the strength he had remaining in his legs. Hawk didn't leap very high, but it was just enough to clear the surface and put him on top of the tumbling snow.

But the loose snow didn't take long to overcome Hawk, burying him beneath it. He came to a halt, stuck in place as the rumbling continued. After about fifteen seconds, which felt like fifteen minutes, the snow stopped.

"You all right?" Hawk asked over the coms.

Nothing.

"Black, are you there?" Hawk asked.

Still nothing.

"Alex, can you hear me?" he called.

She didn't respond either.

Hawk took a deep breath and went over the protocol for surviving an avalanche. He needed to carve out a pocket in front of his face to breathe, a task that sounded easy in theory but far more difficult in practice. With one arm held high above his head, he was able to create a pocket of air. However, moving either of his arms in any direction was challenging given the weight and pressure of the snow. He took several minutes to inch his arm down into position to shovel snow aside in front of his face.

Next, Hawk activated his avalanche beacon sewn into the pocket of his coat. He wasn't sure how deep he was buried, but it was far enough beneath the surface that he couldn't dig his way out. At this point, all he could do was hope and pray Alex would find him soon.

* * *

HAWK'S CONCEPT OF TIME was distorted while stuck like a fly in the ointment. With nothing to do other than think, he felt helpless—and Hawk concluded this was a punishment worse than death itself. To die while being encased in snow would be an ironic end for such a seasoned warrior. Hawk always imagined going out in an epic gun battle or sacrificing himself on a mission to prevent a nuclear detonation. Technically, he was on a mission, but it wasn't one he would consider successful. And his death wouldn't result in anyone's salvation.

Come on, Alex. Where are you?

Hawk's mental state began to deteriorate as another half hour passed. He tried the coms again.

"Alex? Black? Can either of you hear me?"

There was no response.

Hawk had just about given up when he heard a faint but familiar voice calling overhead.

"Hawk! Where are you?"

It was Alex.

"Alex! Alex! I'm down here. Can you hear me?" he said.

She didn't respond, continuing her call.

"Hawk! Where are you? Can you reach the surface?"

He sighed, still helpless to do anything. She was just a few meters away or maybe even standing right on top of him, yet there was no way for him to signal to her his exact location.

Think, Hawk. Think.

While he knew the most important thing for him to do was to conserve his energy, Hawk figured it wouldn't matter if he ended up dead. He worked his hand into his pocket and pulled out his knife. Slowly he inched it up to his other hand before carving into the snow to create a wider circumference around the space where his arm had been.

"I'm down right here," Hawk cried.

"Hawk!" Alex cried.

He heard Alex begin digging above him. In a matter of minutes, she had cleared a large passageway for him to get fresh air.

"Hang in there," she said.

"Have I told you lately how awesome you are?"

She continued digging for another minute or so until all the snow was removed above him. Then she worked on raking snow away from his upper torso until he could also help dig his way out.

They embraced and shed a few tears together.

"As much as I want to hold you tight and never let you go," Hawk said, "we still need to find Black."

"His beacon is activated, but it's not easy to pinpoint the exact location," she said.

"We were about fifty meters apart," Hawk said. "But we were almost parallel with one another."

"That's a place to start," she said.

They estimated that distance and started calling for Black. Hawk froze when he thought he heard him.

"Sshh," Hawk said, holding up his hand in a gesture for Alex to stop. "Listen."

They both heard the faint cries beneath the surface.

"I think we're practically standing on top of him," Hawk said.

They both fell to their knees and started digging. After about a minute of digging, Hawk saw Black's hand, which was still extended upward. Hawk gave it a squeeze before frantically digging with Alex to get his colleague out.

Black collapsed once he reached the surface, a wide grin spread across his face. "I thought you would never find me."

"Well, we weren't going to just leave you here," Hawk said.

Black sat up. "No, she wasn't going to just leave us here." He turned toward Alex. "Do you ever get tired of saving Hawk?"

Alex laughed, but Hawk cast a wary glance at Black.

"This is a two-way street," Hawk said. "It's what being partners is all about in the field."

Black was still grinning. "Just for fun: Alex, can you tell me what the count is on how many times you've saved him to how many times he's saved you?"

"I think I'm ahead eight to five at this point."

Hawk scowled. "Eight to five? Are you mad?"

Alex and Black both shared a laugh at Hawk's expense as they all piled onto Alex's snowmobile before navigating back to the van.

"Now what?" Alex asked. "I know you two have been encased in snow and probably weren't thinking about Obsidian's plant, but it was incinerated before the entrance was covered by falling boulders. And unless you tied up Mack Walsh and left him somewhere, we're back to no leads."

"I almost had Walsh but lost him just before the facility exploded," Hawk said. "But I have a plan."

"Oh?" Black said. "You mind sharing that with the rest of us?"

"We're not going to go looking for Walsh," Hawk said.

"That's quite the plan, Hawk. How exactly do you expect to track down the Obsidian agent without looking for him?"

A faint smile spread across Hawk's lips. "I don't have to look for him because he's going to come looking for us."

"And what makes you so sure of that?" Alex said.

"We're going to turn the tables on him."

CHAPTER 20

Two Days Later
Santa Fe, New Mexico

HAWK ADJUSTED HIS SUNGLASSES before knocking on the adobe bungalow situated in a cul-de-sac at the end of an older neighborhood. Alex stood next to him in a blue dress. She reached up and adjusted his tie.

"You ready?" he asked.

She nodded. "But for the record, I don't think this is a good idea."

"Walsh thought this was my weakness—and the weakness you see in others is often the same weakness you see in yourself."

"There are other ways to doing this," she said.

"We can't afford to wait, and you know it. This is a matter of national security, and sometimes you have to take extreme measures."

After the team left Idaho, Blunt called them to report that the FBI was working in conjunction with

Homeland Security to determine what was going on in Obsidian's mountain facility. While Blunt admitted that he wasn't sure he'd be able to trust any report that emerged from the scene given Obsidian's penchant for co-opting government officials at every level, it would take weeks to remove the rocks blocking the entrance just to get inside. The combination of the explosion and the avalanche rendered the mountain nearly impenetrable for the foreseeable future. Officials were already estimated it would be early summer before the snow would melt and enable them to get the equipment necessary to move the rocks away from the site. And if the Phoenix Foundation was going to find out what Obsidian's plan was to execute its endgame, they couldn't sit around.

"Like I said, there are other ways."

Hawk shot her a glance and knocked.

"You're still letting your emotions get the best of you," she said. "This isn't you, Hawk."

Once he heard footsteps near the door, he reached behind his back and wrapped his hand around his gun.

The door swung open seconds later, revealing a woman with solid gray hair neatly cropped against her face. The wrinkles around the corners of her eyes along with her leathery skin made her look precisely how old Hawk knew she was. At age sixty-seven,

Marsha Templeton was in good health—and naïve about what her son was up to.

"Mrs. Templeton," Hawk said. "We need to have a word with you."

"Okay," she said. "If you're trying to sell me something, I'm not interested."

Hawk brandished his weapon and gestured for her to go back inside. "We just want to talk."

Hawk and Alex strode into the house before Alex shut the door behind them. Wide-eyed and mouth agape, Mrs. Templeton backpedaled into the house.

"What do you want?" she asked. "I'll—I'll give you anything. Money? My car? You want jewelry?"

"Sit down," Hawk said, gesturing toward the couch with his gun, which he then slipped into the back of his pants. "We're not here to hurt you. We just need to talk."

Mrs. Templeton cocked her head to one side and furrowed her brow. "Talk? That's all you want to do? I can do that."

Alex sat down in a chair across from Mrs. Templeton. "We need to talk about your son."

Mrs. Templeton rolled her eyes and let out an exasperated sigh. "What's he done now? Are you with the mafia, needing me to pay off some of his gambling debts? I always told him that betting on sports was going to be the death of him."

Hawk sat down on the love seat and shook his head. "No, Mrs. Templeton, we're not here to collect on a gambling debt. But what your son has done is most definitely going be the death of him."

"Are you the one who's going to kill him?" she asked.

"Only if I have to, but you can help him by helping us."

Hawk glanced at her ringer finger, her wedding band still firmly secured to her hand even though her fourth husband had been dead for a couple of years. Despite knowing her story, Hawk wanted to see what kind of woman he was dealing with.

"Have you recently remarried?" Hawk asked.

She shook her head. "I can't bring myself to let go of Ned. He was such a good man to me."

"Is that why he beat you?"

She scowled at Hawk. "You seem to know an awful lot about me, yet you said that you're here to talk about my son."

"We are," Alex said, intervening with a gentle touch. "My partner can get a little sidetracked from time to time."

"The reason we're here is to learn more about your son because of what he's done," Hawk said. "And I happen to think it might be related to all your dead husbands. I mean, your next husband should have serious reservations about marrying a woman whose previous four husbands have all been murdered."

"What are you suggesting, Mr.—"

"Mr. Flannigan will suffice," Hawk said.

"What are you suggesting, Mr. Flannigan?"

"I'm not suggesting anything. This is a direct question. Is your son the one who is killing all of your husbands? I read about how your first husband, Grant Walsh—the father of your son—died in an accident while hiking on a trip in the Grand Canyon."

"Accidents happen," she said, remaining evasive.

Hawk continued his attempts to get her to crack. "I also know you had filed to divorce him and he had employed one of the toughest divorce lawyers in Los Angeles to make sure you got as little as possible."

"Is there a point to all this, Mr. Flannigan?"

"You tell me," Hawk fired back. "Why do all your husbands—albeit abusive ones—die in some strange accident that could very well be interpreted as murder?"

"If you know so much about me, you'd know that I've always been more or less cursed," she said. "Like when my parents died when our house exploded due to a gas leak."

"Seems like your luck was pretty good since you were sleeping at a friend's house that night."

"Or that my first baby was kidnapped and I never saw him again."

"And the next week you were driving a new car," Hawk said. "The black market for babies was pretty lucrative during those days."

"If you're with the government, why don't you go ahead and arrest me since you've already convicted me in your own mind. It'd save us a whole lot of time bantering about this."

"What he means to say," Alex said, placing her hand on top of Mrs. Templeton's, "is that we're sorry for all the incredible loss you've suffered in your life. We can't make it go away, but we want you to avoid experiencing any more excruciating pain."

Mrs. Templeton sighed and looked up before turning her gaze toward Alex. "So, what do you want to know about my Mack?"

"Have you spoken with him lately?" Alex asked.

Mrs. Templeton shrugged. "I don't know what you would consider recently, but I did have a conversation with him on the phone last week. He told me to be careful and that he probably shouldn't have done what he did."

"Did he give you any details?" Alex asked.

"No, but I just figured it was his usual mischief. Nothing too serious."

Alex nodded. "Is this something he did often?"

"At least once every few months," Mrs. Templeton said. "It's like he's worried somebody's going to show up at my house with a gun and shoot me."

"I didn't come here to shoot you, Mrs. Templeton," Hawk said as he narrowed his eyes. "I'm not half the animal your son when he gutted my mother like an savage and left her body on her front porch, using her blood to write a message and get my attention."

"But you're definitely here threatening me," she said before breaking into a coughing fit.

Hawk glanced at the pack of cigarettes on the coffee table. "Need a smoke break?"

She nodded.

"Then let's take this to the back porch," Hawk said. "You don't have any snoopy neighbors, do you?"

"What other kind is there?" she said with a chuckle. "They're all at work right now. We won't have to worry about them."

They followed Mrs. Templeton to the back porch. Hawk didn't want to continue the conversation outside without doing his due diligence. He searched the perimeter, peeking his head over the top of the privacy fence in all three directions to make sure there wasn't anyone lurking who could eavesdrop on their conversation. Once satisfied that the area was free of any bystanders, he sat down.

"So Mack finally crossed the line, huh?" Mrs. Templeton said before flicking her lighter and igniting a cigarette.

Hawk nodded. "I'd be surprised if this was the first time. Maybe the first time you heard about it though."

Mrs. Templeton shrugged. "I should've seen it coming. You never want to believe the worst about your own kid. Everybody else's kids are the problem, but not your own. And even when deep down you know they are, you can justify their actions and make excuses for them. It's what we do best as the human race. We have loads of grace for our family and zero tolerance for others."

"Look, I know I may not have gone about this the right way," Hawk said. "But I need your help. There is a serious threat not only to our country but to the rest of the world—and Mack is the only link we have right now to the people who are behind this."

"My Mack? He's an evil villain who's going to destroy the world?" she asked before laughing, which quickly devolved into another coughing fit.

"I'm not sure how much he knows about what he's doing," Hawk said. "But he knows enough to understand how dangerous things are. And he's obviously unhinged since he's now out slashing throats at the behest of his employer."

"If all this stuff that you're telling me is true, what do you want me to do about it? It's not like he ever listened to me in the first place."

"We want you to ask him to come home," Alex said.

Mrs. Templeton shook her head. "He won't do it. He's too busy with whatever it is that he's doing. He only visits me during the holidays, and they won't be rolling around again for quite some time."

"I think it's pretty obvious that he loves his mother," Hawk said. "You just need to give him a good reason to see you."

"Like what?" she asked.

"Perhaps that you just found out you have cancer and only have a few weeks to live," Hawk said. "That should spur him back quickly."

"If I tell him that, he'll never believe me again for as long as I live."

Alex rested her hand reassuringly on Mrs. Templeton's forearm. "If this organization isn't stopped, none of us may live much longer."

Mrs. Templeton sighed before taking a long drag on her cigarette. She sent a plume of smoke towering upward before responding.

"I don't like the idea of being used as your bait, Mr. Flannigan," she said. "And I don't like the way you've implicated my son in the murder of your mother. But I'll do it. I'll tell him I've got cancer with only weeks to live in order to get him to come back home. However, I must warn you that he could also come here with a whole army of thugs if he gets suspicious about anything."

"We'll be ready for anything he throws at us," Hawk said.

"Just promise me you won't kill him," she said.

"I'm not sure I can—"

"If you do have to kill him," Mrs. Templeton interrupted, "please don't do it in front of me."

"We'll do our best not to," Alex said. "But it's hard to make those promises without knowing what the future holds."

"I understand. Just do your best, okay?" Mrs. Templeton said.

Hawk nodded and stood along with Alex, and they followed Mrs. Templeton into her house. Once they reached the kitchen, Mrs. Templeton took the phone off the hook and dialed her son's number.

Taking a few steps back to give her space, Hawk watched Mrs. Templeton as she spoke with her son. She wasn't anything like Hawk's mother, though not many women were. But there was a familiar trait he noticed, one inherent in all mothers.

Mrs. Templeton cared about her son.

As she talked, Hawk noticed how her voice softened and her eyes lit up. Even the most cynical person could see that she cherished her son. Whatever misfortune she had experienced didn't seem to dampen the joy she exuded when speaking with Mack. Her eyes twinkled, and the corners of her mouth seemed to be permanently etched upward.

But then her face fell.

"There's something I need to tell you, son," she said. "And it's serious. I've only got a few weeks to live." A tear trickled down her face before she sniffled. "I want you to come see me as soon as you can, okay?"

Seconds later, mascara-streaked tears were rolling down her cheeks as her eyes turned red as she hung up the phone.

"He'll be here tomorrow," she said before shuffling into the living room and collapsing on the couch.

Alex walked over to Hawk. "I told you this wasn't the right way to go about this. Look what you've done to this poor woman."

"I probably should've listened to you," Hawk said, "but what's done is done. Now we just have to watch her every move until he gets here."

CHAPTER 21

AN HOUR AFTER MRS. TEMPLETON delivered the news to Mack, he called the house again and asked if he could meet her at their spot the next morning at 10:00 a.m. He said he was flying in but had a little surprise for her.

"Where's your special place?" Hawk asked.

Mrs. Templeton ignited another cigarette and didn't respond until she cycled smoke through her lungs and out her nose.

"There's an overlook in the Santa Fe National Forest that we used to go to all the time when he was a kid," she said. "We didn't have much money, so we went hiking all the time as opposed to having him sit in front of the television playing shoot-'em-up video games. A lot of good that did."

"Anything in particular you can tell us about this overlook?" Alex asked.

"I have plenty of pictures," she said. "Would you like to see them?"

Hawk and Alex both nodded.

Mrs. Templeton walked over to a bookshelf and selected a photo album.

"I know you young people may have never seen one of these," Mrs. Templeton said, "but this is how we used to look at pictures back when we developed them into prints and didn't have them on our phones."

Hawk smiled at the woman's wit. She was growing on him.

After she took a seat, he and Alex sat on Mrs. Templeton's left and right, respectively. She opened up the book and thumbed through the pages, skipping through several until she reached a page full of pictures of the overlook.

"It's just beautiful up there," she said. "Mack told me that he always felt so tall and invincible when we went up to El Diablo Point."

"It's called El Diablo Point?" Alex asked.

"Yes, the local Spanish settlers called it that because they thought it was the kind of place the devil would've taken Jesus to tempt him, like the story in the Bible. You can see all of Santa Fe from that vantage point."

"So it's a popular spot?" Alex asked.

Mrs. Templeton shook her head. "It's a rather difficult hike."

"Can you still make it?" Hawk asked.

"It'll take me longer than usual, but I can still hoof it up the mountain without too many issues."

Hawk asked for directions to the bathroom and excused himself.

"Are you getting all this?" he asked over the coms.

"Loud and clear," Black said. "I'll make a little trip up to El Diablo Point right away since I don't suspect you're tempted to leave."

"I'm warming up to this woman," Hawk said, "but I still don't trust her."

"Can't say that I blame you, though her sobbing sounded pretty genuine."

"There's no doubt that she's scared, but I think she's manufacturing some of this."

"Just wait until she turns out to be Mother Theresa."

Hawk chuckled. "If she is, Alex will have my hide. She's already upset about how things went down."

"You could've approached the woman in a less threatening manner."

"How would you have done it?"

"Same way you did," Black said. "Though I probably wouldn't have even mentioned anything about the gun to Alex beforehand and let it be a surprise to her too."

"You're going to have a hard time with marriage," Hawk said.

"I'm not trying to get married here. We're trying to catch a man who might be able to help us stop a virus that will wipe out half the world's population."

"Fair enough. Now when you get back from El Diablo Point, call me so we can discuss the lay of the land. I don't want any surprises tomorrow."

"Roger that."

* * *

HAWK CHOSE TO BACK OFF and let Alex work her magic with Mrs. Templeton. While Alex often bucked authority, she had a tender side that could win over even the coldest of hearts in little to no time at all. Offering to help or being attentive to a person's needs, she could make another person feel like he or she was the most important soul in the room. That trait was also one that endeared her to Hawk.

In an effort to stay out of the way, Hawk flipped through a collection of magazines on the coffee table, most of them focusing on the beauty of the Santa Fe. There was little doubt that Mrs. Templeton enjoyed living there and was indeed proud of her hometown. She had held several creative jobs over the years, working for a local communications company. Everything from a photographer to a graphic designer and plenty of jobs in between filled up her resume.

But it was her most recent job, the one she'd taken after she officially retired, that caught Hawk's attention.

She was a trail guide at the Santa Fe National Forest before her knees started acting up—at least, that's what she told Hawk and Alex. If anyone knew their way around the area, Mrs. Templeton did.

"So I imagine you've been to El Diablo point many times," Hawk said.

"Of course," she said.

"In that case, can you draw me a rudimentary map of the area and show me what I can see from the top of the point?"

"Sure," she said as she began scribbling onto a piece of paper. As she used her art skills to sketch out El Diablo Point, she penciled in labels on certain portions that could be viewed from that height. In a matter of minutes, Hawk had a good idea what was in store for them in the morning.

* * *

AFTER SHARING A PIZZA they had delivered, Mrs. Templeton said that she wanted to go to bed. Alex asked if she could sleep on the floor in Mrs. Templeton's room.

"Are you afraid that I'm going somewhere?" she asked.

Alex shook her head. "No, not at all. I just

thought it might be a better way to ensure that we all get a good night of sleep and you're not worried that we're going to storm in here and shoot you. That's all."

"You could storm in here in the middle of the night and shoot me?" Mrs. Templeton asked.

"That's not going to happen," Alex said reassuringly. "That was just a poor choice of words. Especially after the way we got off on the wrong foot coming in here with blazing guns. I'm just thankful that you're helping us and see your assistance for what it really is—the heart of someone who deeply cares about the fabric of our society."

"I don't think I've ever heard anyone put it in those terms, but I would say that's fairly accurate. I love my son, but if he's involved in something this sinister, I can't allow that."

"I know," Alex said. "As difficult as it might be for you, you're doing the right thing."

Mrs. Templeton smiled and then said she was going to the bathroom.

"Of course," Alex said. "Take your time. Take all the time that you need."

Alex crept into the hallway to connect with Hawk one final time before bed.

"How are things going back there?" he asked.

"Fine as far as I can tell," Alex said, keeping her voice low.

"You trust her?"

Alex sighed. "I don't know. She seems pretty sincere. I guess we'll find out tomorrow."

"Do you think you can handle her if I leave you two alone?" Hawk asked. "Black and I need to discuss plans for tomorrow. He went up to El Diablo Point and scoped it out for us this afternoon."

"I'm good. You go on. I've got this."

Hawk kissed his wife on the cheek. "Be careful."

* * *

HAWK EASED OUTSIDE, pulling the door shut behind him. He scanned the area but didn't see Black.

"Where are you?" Hawk asked over the coms. "I just finished up inside and thought we could plan for tomorrow now that you've been up there to take a look at it."

"I'm getting takeout at a Chinese place up the street here," Black said. "You want me to get you something?"

"I've already eaten," Hawk said. "But thanks for the offer. When will you be back?"

"Five or ten minutes, depending on how long it takes them to make my food."

"Okay, I'll be outside taking a little walk."

"Roger that," Black said.

Hawk paced back and forth in front of the residence along the sidewalk for a minute or two before a pair of men jumped out of a black SUV and grabbed him. He tried to fight back, but one of the men snatched Hawk's gun while the other man jammed a taser into Hawk's neck and then yanked the com units out of his ear.

"You're coming with us," one of the men growled.

CHAPTER 22

TWO MEN DRAGGED Hawk into their SUV before a driver stomped on the gas and sped away from the house. After a couple minutes, Hawk regained consciousness and realized his hands were tied behind his back.

"What's going on?" he asked.

"Why don't you tell us," the man next to Hawk said.

"Who are you?"

"Lester Sanders, FBI," the man said as he displayed his badge. "Those men are Special Agents Baker and Underhill. And we know who you are."

Hawk sighed. "I doubt that because if you knew who I was, you wouldn't dare try to interfere with what I'm working on and would stay the hell away."

"We took a picture of you and ran it through the federal database," Sanders said. "Apparently, we don't have access to your file, but we know you're in there."

"My identity needs to be kept a secret," Hawk

said. "I'm sure you can appreciate that."

"That doesn't change the fact that you're treading into our territory here," Baker said.

"I'm only going to warn you once more," Hawk fired back. "I'd hate for you gentlemen to be caught up in the crossfire."

"There's no crossfire here," Baker said. "You're just screwing up our operation."

"And what operation is that?" Hawk asked. "Because whatever it is, I can guarantee you that it's not nearly as important as the one I'm on."

"Smuggling," Sanders said. "Or more specifically, smuggling women across the border and selling them to traffickers."

"We've been following this woman for months and almost have enough on her to put her away for years and put an end to this illegal ring," Baker said.

"That is until you butted in earlier today," Sanders said with a snarl.

Hawk shook his head. "Look, I know you think what you're doing is important and that it's the right thing—and it might be. But I swear that if I told you what I was doing—which I can't—you'd abandon your stakeout in a New York minute and let me proceed with what we're doing with Mrs. Templeton."

"All our work will go down the drain if you try to pull this stunt on us," Sanders said. "You have to at least try and see things from our perspective."

"I could try, but it'd be a waste of my time and yours," Hawk said. "The reality is we're talking about millions of people dying if you pull me off this operation."

"Sorry, Slugger," Sanders said. "We're going to put you on the sideline until tomorrow at noon when we bust that old lady's trafficking ring."

"Sorry," Hawk said. "No can do. You can have her after I get through with her tomorrow morning. What we're doing doesn't even really involve her but her son, but I can't tell you anything more."

"Doesn't look like you're in a position of leverage, now does it?" Sanders said. "And if you're not going to cooperate, we're going to make sure that you do."

"And how's that?" Hawk asked.

"We're going to detain you at one of our black sites," Baker said.

Hawk shook his head. "That's not a good idea."

Sanders chuckled. "Whatever, mystery federal agent. We'll take our chances."

Hawk eased his hands, which were tied behind him, over to the seatbelt latch and slowly depressed the button. Once he was free, he put his shoulder into Sanders and drove him against the SUV door. For good measure, he smashed his head into the window twice, rendering him unconscious.

Baker, who was sitting in the passenger seat in the front, didn't react quickly enough. Hawk smashed his hands over a sharp portion of the console in the front, breaking his hands free. Then he grabbed Baker's seatbelt and yanked hard against it, pinning him against his seat.

Underhill went for his firearm, but Hawk reached down with his free hand to pull Sanders's gun out of its holster. Hawk clicked off the safety.

"I suggest you keep your hands on the wheel where I can see them and just drive to the black site," Hawk directed.

Underhill eased his hands back onto the steering wheel and drove on for several minutes until they reached the old warehouse.

"You put that gun where I can see it," Hawk said.

Underhill slowly complied.

"That's it," Hawk said. "Nice and easy. We don't need to make a mess out of things over jurisdiction, especially since you'd lose."

Sanders moaned and was starting to regain consciousness before Hawk pistol-whipped the FBI agent in the head, knocking him out again.

Hawk led the two men inside and secured them with zip ties to a pair of weight-bearing poles a good ten meters apart from each other. While Hawk never wanted to disparage federal agents, he didn't appreciate getting tasered by Sanders. Instead of kindly hoisting the man over his shoulder, Hawk wanted to drag Sanders through the gravel parking lot before tying him to a tree.

But that was too far, despite Hawk's feelings of being disrespected and condescended to. Hawk picked up Sanders and carted him into the warehouse before setting him down at the base of another nearby pole. Once Sanders was secure, Hawk searched all three of the FBI agents. Satisfied that they weren't going anywhere, he paced around the room.

"Believe me when I say this," Hawk started, "because it is with all sincerely I confess that I didn't want to do this. However, you forced my hand. And as a result, you can thank me later. Now, I must be off, but I promise you that the moment I am through conducting my operation, I'll notify someone of your location and have you cut free."

Hawk hustled back to the SUV and returned to Mrs. Templeton's bungalow. He pulled to a stop behind Black's vehicle. Stooping down, Hawk tapped on the window, gesturing for Black to unlock the door.

"Where have you been?" Black asked. "I thought something happened to you. I tried raising you on the coms and everything."

"Unlock the door, and I'll tell you what happened."

Black complied and stared wide-eyed at Hawk. "Take a tumble there, big fella?"

"More like a rumble with some federal agents."

"Are you kidding me?"

Hawk shook his head. "I wish I was. Apparently, Mrs. Templeton isn't the saint she portrays herself to be. And based on what those agents said, she's involved in some sort of human trafficking ring by smuggling illegals over the border."

"A National Forest is a great place to hide people," Black said.

"Whatever that woman is up to, it's not good. And I'm really concerned for Alex now."

"She can handle herself."

"I'm not worried about that," Hawk said. "It just seems to me that the apple doesn't fall far from the tree. I'm starting to wonder if she didn't give Walsh some kind of signal when she spoke."

"We'll be ready tomorrow," Black said. "Let me show you how we're going to handle the situation."

CHAPTER 23

THE NEXT MORNING, Hawk awoke to the smell of coffee brewing and bacon sizzling in a frying pan. He looked at his watch with one eye open and then glanced toward the window. It was still dark outside at just a shade past 6:30 a.m.

He groaned and sank back into the couch. "What's going on? Do you realize what time it is?"

"I sure do, sweetie," Mrs. Templeton said as she tousled Hawk's hair. "Your wife and I woke up with a little spring in our step, and she thought it'd be a great idea to make breakfast for everyone."

"Well, I do operate better on a full stomach, that's for sure," Hawk said, forcing a smile as he lumbered toward the table.

He wanted to take a plate to Black and felt a little guilty for eating so well. Meanwhile, Black was probably going to have to woof down a fast food breakfast burrito from somewhere. But Hawk wanted to keep Black's presence a surprise, especially in light of what he learned about Mrs. Templeton from the FBI agents.

Alex made some eggs and toast, serving as side items for the bacon. Hawk was grateful for the meal and profusely thanked both women before taking a quick shower. Once he got dressed, he questioned Mrs. Templeton again the logistics of getting to El Diablo Point.

"It'll take us about an hour and a half at this time in the morning, counting traffic and the hike to the spot," she said.

"Then we need to get moving," Hawk said. "I want to get there at least a half hour early to make sure that we have all our bases covered."

She snatched her pack of cigarettes off the table and packed them. Using her tongue, she wrangled one out of the box before igniting the tobacco.

"It's your show," she said. "Me and my cancer are just along for the ride."

Hawk nodded. "I just want to warn you that I might say some unsavory things about you today when your son arrives, but just know that I'm only doing it to extract information from him."

"Don't fool yourself, Mr. Flannigan. You just want revenge like everybody else. You couldn't care less about justice. I've seen your type. You just want to pump Mack full of lead and fool yourself into believing that the problem has been solved."

"You don't know the first thing about me or what drives all my decisions."

"I know it's not justice, at least not in this case. My son is likely some low-level grunt, doing the bidding of far more powerful people. Yet, you're targeting him like the whole system is going crumble if he goes down. It won't. They'll just slide someone else into his place and carry on."

Hawk sighed. "Convince him to work with us. I know you can do that."

"Mack is as stubborn as they come, just like his father was," she said.

"What really happened to Mack's father?"

"I told you that he died."

"How did he die?" Hawk asked. "Or better yet, how did Mack kill him?"

"I never said Mack killed him," she said.

"But your face did. What did your first husband do? Beat you? Yell at you? Degrade you? I'm sure it was justified."

Mrs. Templeton narrowed her eyes. "He died, okay? Mack didn't have anything to do with it."

"So you say," Hawk said. "But I know different. Did he help you with your other three husbands as well?"

"Don't you dare suggest anything like that ever

again," Mrs. Templeton said. "I'll report you for kidnapping me to the local authorities. And if you want to talk about justice, I know a half dozen judges here who'd do whatever I say."

Hawk nodded.

A half-dozen judges who you're paying off to get these girls through the system.

"Fine," he said. "I'll call a truce on this, but I swear to you that if things go south today, you'll be the one getting the brunt of it. Don't think your son is going to save you somehow. Just go along with our plan, and we'll leave you alone forever after this morning. Got it?"

"Understood," she said with a sneer.

"Now grab your keys and let's go," Hawk said. "We're taking your car."

* * *

EL DIABLO POINT overlooked the valley, and Hawk instantly realized how the location received its name. Anyone who stood on the rock that jutted out from the cliff could see for miles—and feel like royalty overlooking a kingdom.

Hawk climbed up on the boulder and peered out across the land. He looked through his binoculars at the parking lot and gave a subtle signal to Black, who had followed them there. He set up a perimeter alarm along the trail, giving Hawk and Alex a heads up that someone was heading toward them. Once everything was in place, Black was supposed to join them a few minutes before the scheduled rendezvous.

Hawk took Mrs. Templeton's phone and handed it to Alex. "She'll be in charge of your cell until your son arrives. I'm sure you understand."

Mrs. Templeton nodded. "I find it hard to believe that you don't trust me."

"You shouldn't take it personally, Mrs. Templeton. I don't trust anyone."

At 9:55 a.m., Black strode into the clearing at El Diablo Point and joined them.

"Who's this?" Mrs. Templeton asked, her wild eyes wide with fear.

"Just a friend," Alex said. "You don't have anything to be afraid of."

"Has he been here the whole time, just lurking in the trees?"

"He just got here, but he's going to help us ensure that everything goes smoothly."

Mrs. Templeton lit another cigarette and took a long drag before continuing the conversation. "Mack's not gonna like this. He'll be like a caged animal—a caged and wounded animal."

"We'll be able to handle him," Hawk said. "Just play it cool, okay? I don't want you getting hurt during this whole ordeal."

At ten minutes past 10:00 a.m., Walsh had yet to arrive. The perimeter alarm had been tripped twice, but both times Black checked his phone to see the images transmitted back to him. One was of two young women hiking, while the other was an elderly couple.

"Still no sign of him," Hawk said softly to Black. "Maybe we overestimated Walsh's affection for his mother."

While they were talking, Mrs. Templeton gasped and let out a short cry.

"You made it," she said, her gaze trained on the front of El Diablo Point.

Hawk spun and looked toward the front of the rock and watched Mack Walsh scramble to his feet and pull his gun. Hawk trained his weapon on Mack as he darted behind Mrs. Templeton.

"That's far enough," Hawk said. "Put the gun down."

Walsh, who was sporting a Kevlar vest and a helmet, had yet to remove his rock climbing harness and breathed heavily after summiting the rock face.

"Is this how you want to play it?" Walsh asked. "I kill your mother, then you kill mine? I don't know what you think is going to come of this, but you're not going to learn anything. There are people far more powerful than you ever imagined, people in our own government, pulling the strings here. And if you think threatening to kill my mother is going to change things, you're dead wrong."

"You're outgunned," Black said. "There are only two ways this ends, and you won't be pleased with either one."

Walsh laughed as he unbuckled his harness and shook it off onto the ground. "This is a joke, right? We both know you're not going to kill my mother."

"Don't test me," Hawk said. "I know what kind of woman she is. And it wouldn't be hard to pull the trigger."

"I doubt that. Whatever you know, she's far worse."

Mrs. Templeton glared at her son. "That's rich coming from you."

"Says my sick and dying mother," Walsh shot back. "I knew that was a lie the moment you told me. All those fake tears? Was that for these agents here or for me?"

"At least I had the decency to warn you. Maybe that was a mistake, especially if you're going to talk about me like that?" she said. "How dare you!"

"Put a sock in it, old lady," Walsh said. "You told me there was only one agent to worry about, not two."

"That's right," Black said. "There's no way out of this for you."

"Do I look concerned?" Walsh asked.

"If you knew this was a trap, why'd you come?" Hawk asked. "Is Obsidian really that concerned about one agent?"

Walsh shook his head. "I'm just following orders."

"So am I," Hawk countered.

"You're wasting your time because no matter what you do to me, you won't be able to stop them," Walsh said. "They are moving ahead regardless of whether I'm alive or dead."

"At this point, do you think I really care about that?" Hawk said. "I want justice for my mother."

"And you're going to get that my shooting my mother?" Walsh asked. "Come on, Hawk. This isn't you. Let me save you the trouble."

Walsh took aim at his mother, firing twice. Realizing what Walsh was doing, Hawk pushed Mrs. Templeton to the side, but it was too late. One bullet ripped through her chest while the other grazed her side.

Hawk and Black both fired back but they didn't have much of a target to aim for as Walsh dove off the side of the cliff.

CHAPTER 24

HAWK KNELT DOWN next to Mrs. Templeton and propped her head up. He tried to stop the bleeding, applying pressure with his hands. Alex handed him a sweatshirt to help, but the blood flow wasn't slowing down fast enough.

"It's all right," Mrs. Templeton said as she gasped for air. "I deserve this."

"No one deserves to be murdered by their own son," Hawk said.

"I had it coming one way or another," she said before coughing up some more blood.

"Please," Hawk said, "if you know anything about what he's planning on doing, tell us now. You might be able to help save innocent lives."

She coughed some more and struggled to take a deep breath before closing her eyes.

"Mrs. Templeton, stay with us," Alex said, taking the woman's hand.

She opened her eyes again, barely wide enough

to see her pupils.

"He texted me that he was going to kill you and return to Washington for one more job and then he was getting out."

"Thank you, Mrs. Templeton," Hawk said.

"If you see him again, tell him I love him," she said.

Her body fell limp in Hawk's arms.

Alex closed her eyes and shook her head. "She's gone."

"What a bastard," Hawk said. "He just killed his own mother. One more job? Yeah, right."

Black hustled back over to Hawk and Alex. "She didn't make it, did she?"

"She didn't have a prayer," Hawk said.

"Well, Walsh made it," Black said. "He pulled a chute and made it safely to the ground near the parking lot before he tore out of here."

"How were they communicating?" Black asked. "I thought you confiscated her phone."

"We did," Alex said. "Apparently, she had another one."

Alex searched Mrs. Templeton's pockets and found a cell phone. "Would you look at this?"

The device was password protected and prevented Alex from getting into the data.

"Use her thumbprint to the open the phone," Hawk said. "It's still turned on, isn't it?"

"It is, but this cell uses facial recognition," she said.

"Try it," Black said.

Alex held the phone in front of Mrs. Templeton, allowing it to scan her face. The phone buzzed and opened up.

"Bingo," Alex said and started to look for the text exchange between Mrs. Templeton and her son.

"There's nothing here," Alex said. "All the texts have been deleted."

"Can you retrieve any of it another way?" Hawk asked.

"Yeah, but that'd take more time than we have."

"You're right," Hawk said. "We're low on time anyway since I have to circle back and explain all this to the FBI."

"FBI?" Alex asked.

"I didn't have a chance to tell you," Hawk said. "But it doesn't matter now. Some feds jumped me last night in front of the house, apprehending me to keep me away from Mrs. Templeton."

"But you're here," she said. "What did you do?"

Hawk grimaced. "I broke free and sort of tied them up at one of their black sites."

"Oh, Hawk," she said. "And now Mrs. Templeton is dead."

"And we need to get back to Washington," Hawk said. "I'll drop by and release them and give them a quick rundown of what happened. In the meantime, you two need to get to the airport and get the plane ready."

"What business could Walsh have in Washington?" Black asked.

"The National Security Complex dedication," Alex said. "That's happening tomorrow afternoon."

Hawk's eyes widened. "Who all is going to be there?"

"Everybody," she said. "All of Washington will be there to celebrate the opening of the facility."

Hawk nodded. "We better hurry."

CHAPTER 25

HAWK'S BRIEF RETURN to the FBI black site wasn't a pleasant one as he delivered the news of Mrs. Templeton's death before freeing all of the agents. Sanders was livid and promised that they would seek retribution for Hawk meddling with their operation. After apologizing a second time for how things went down, Hawk volunteered to return in his free time to help crack the smuggling ring. His offer wasn't received all that well, but Hawk didn't concern himself with it as he drove back to the airport. His team had far more pressing matters, the kind with national security implications.

The engines for the Phoenix Foundation's jet whirred as Hawk stepped out of the SUV and onto the tarmac. He hustled over to the plane and joined Alex and Black, who were already settled in. After notifying the pilot that they were ready to depart, Hawk buckled up and closed his eyes for a moment. He needed a chance to process all the chaotic events that had just unfolded along with a plan on how to proceed.

Hawk leaned back and wondered if Walsh was right about trying to take down Obsidian. Perhaps the organization was too powerful and influential to be stopped. Maybe such efforts were a waste of his time. But Hawk refused to accept such a fate. He had to try to do something.

When he felt a gentle touch on his shoulders, he opened his eyes and looked up at Alex.

"You all right?" she asked.

"All things considered, I guess I'm okay," he said.

"How'd your new friends at the FBI take the news about Mrs. Templeton?"

"About as well as you'd expect—livid, angry, upset, and vowing to get back at me somehow."

She smiled. "That wouldn't be the first time."

"You can say that again."

"I just can't help but think how this plan to lure out Walsh led to Mrs. Templeton's death. And we didn't even get him."

Hawk sighed. "I hate that she lost her life, but she sabotaged our entire operation by telling her son what we were doing—and she was trafficking illegal girls in the U.S. Just think about that. Sex trafficking, Alex. She wasn't a good woman."

"But Walsh didn't even try to kill you."

"Maybe he realized it was better to fight another day than to get into a shootout when he was outnumbered. I mean, you have to hand it to him—his plan worked. We were so distracted and confused that he was able to get away. Even worse, if he had any suspicion that we don't want to kill him, that episode this morning confirmed it for him. Our agenda is out in the open now, and he'll be able to use that to his advantage."

"Our agenda is stopping Obsidian no matter what," Alex said. "But maybe we've been approaching this the wrong way."

Hawk sat upright in his chair. "What do you mean?"

"Everything we've been doing is reactive, not proactive. Obsidian is dictating the game."

"Until we know what they're trying to achieve, it's hard to be anything other than reactive," Black said.

"That's why maybe we need to go on the offensive," Alex said. "As much as it'd be nice to catch Walsh—and I know that you need that for closure, Hawk—we need to be more than just a mild pain in their ass. We need to disrupt everything they're doing."

Hawk nodded in agreement. "That sounds like a great plan, but we still need something—anything—to build off of, no matter how weak the connection might be. Outside of Walsh and what we can learn six months from now once we can get back into that Idaho mountain, we're still flying blind. So, we need Walsh now."

"And once we catch him, we start hunting these people one by one," Black said. "After all, we're the assassins here."

The team came to a quick consensus that once they caught Walsh, they would shift gears. But given the gravity of the impending threat at the dedication the next day, they had no choice but to defend all the high-ranking state officials.

Hawk called Blunt and caught him up on the situation as well as the team's desire to warn General Van Fortner about what Obsidian was planning.

"I think that'd be a waste of our time," Blunt said. "Fortner isn't going to cave to a possible terrorist attack. He'd see canceling the event as a sign of weakness. And there's nothing more he wants to do right now that display strength, both as a leader and for the country."

"You should at least tell him," Hawk said. "He has a right to know."

"Right now, I'm wary of telling anyone anything," Blunt said. "The entire intelligence community seems like it's riddled with so many leaks that we're sinking into the abyss."

"So, you're just going to give up like that?"

"Absolutely not," Blunt said. "You're going to prevent that attack from ever taking place and make General Fortner look like the strong leader that he is."

"Just promise me two things."

"Depends on what you want."

"I don't want you on that stage tomorrow, and I want you to warn Fortner in person. Give him a chance to decide what to do for himself."

Blunt grunted. "I'll only agree to one of them."

"Come on, you can tell Fortner," Hawk said.

"That's the one I'm going to attempt," Blunt said with a chuckle.

"But you could be a target. Don't be a fool."

"If Obsidian really considered me a threat, I'd probably be dead already," Blunt said. "But if Fortner decides to move forward anyway, I can't abandon him. What kind of faith would that show in my agents? You and Black are two of the best operatives in the world, or am I mistaken?"

"Just be careful, sir," Hawk said before he hung up. He sighed and slumped into his seat.

"So," Alex began, "what did Blunt say?"

"He said he'd talk to Fortner—and that we better catch Walsh tomorrow and make sure nobody dies."

"I'd expect nothing less from our fearless leader," Black said.

Alex stared with her mouth agape. "He's not

242 | R.J. PATTERSON

going to urge Fortner to cancel the dedication?"

Hawk shook his head. "He's going to let Fortner make that decision, but Blunt acted like that was little more than a courtesy call."

"Of course Fortner is going to hold the ceremony as planned," Black said. "He's a proud Army man and has high expectations for the people he's leading now."

"In that case, let's make sure we don't disappoint Blunt or Fortner tomorrow," Hawk said.

* * *

BLUNT TOOK A SEAT on the park bench in Rock Creek Park, folded up his Washington Post, and tucked it beneath his armpit. He gnawed on a cigar and waited five minutes until a man wearing a dark suit and sunglasses approached from the east. He tightened his scarf and sat down next to Blunt.

"Great day for a walk," the man said.

"Great day to be alive," Blunt answered back.

The man leaned forward, his fingers interlocked in front of him. "He'll be in the white SUV on the northwest corner of the park. Five minutes."

Blunt nodded at the man, who stood and casually strolled away.

After the allotted time, Blunt stood and lumbered toward the Fortner's vehicle. Once inside, Blunt found the director poring over the latest intelligence report.

"What new threats are we facing today?" Blunt asked.

"Nothing new in here," Fortner said without looking up from his documents. "This stuff never changes. Terrorist cells trying to assault American interests abroad. Sleeper cells recruiting heavily on the web. To be honest, I'm really disappointed at the lack of originality these days by those people who are hell bent on bringing America to its knees. This is like amateur hour."

"Well, I've got one for you that I can almost guarantee you haven't read about this week."

Fortner stopped and looked over the top of his glasses. "Something original? Now that would be refreshing."

"I don't think you're going to like this one," Blunt said.

"Try me."

"We have credible intelligence about an attack at tomorrow's National Security Complex dedication."

Fortner furrowed his brow. "Really? Someone has the cajones to make an attempt there?"

"It's very serious."

Fortner chuckled and shook his head. "And I welcome the opportunity to show the strength of American security."

"I'm not sure I would laugh this one off."

Fortner eyed Blunt. "Okay, I'm listening. Who's behind this?"

"Obsidian."

Fortner chuckled again. "I thought you said this was serious."

"I did."

"Well, Obsidian has supposedly been lying in wait for years now, and nothing they're ever supposed to do happens. Just the name Obsidian has become the intelligence community's wolf."

"And I'm sure they would prefer to have it that way," Blunt said. "Tomorrow, there's going to be a strike, and I suggest you heighten the threat level."

"Will your star agents be there?"

"Of course, but—"

"Then I have nothing to worry about, now do I?" Fortner slapped Blunt on his knee with a file folder and nodded toward the door.

"That's it?" Blunt asked.

"I've got a lot to do today in preparation for the big day tomorrow—and apparently, so does your team."

CHAPTER 26

Langley, Virginia
National Security Complex

HAWK PACED AROUND the perimeter of the public area designated as the staging ground for the building dedication. While security was understandably tight, Hawk studied the face of every person he came in contact with working the grounds. The facility had its own set of guards who patrolled outside the gate and inside it as well. On top of that, several senators insisted upon bringing their personal sentries.

"This is a disaster just waiting to happen," Hawk said into his coms. "If something goes down, there will be so much posturing over territory and jurisdiction that by the time they settle who's in charge, the perpetrators will be gone."

"Ain't that the truth," Black said.

Hawk made eye contact with his colleague, who was surveying the other side of the late-arriving media.

Several reporters hustled to set up their equipment in advance of the beginning of the ceremonies. Five minutes before the event was scheduled to start, access to the area was prohibited. An NSC staffer performed a mic check for all the television and radio stations recording the event and received thumbs up gestures from various members of the media.

"This is the two-minute warning," the man said into the microphone before slinking off stage.

"You hear that, Alex?" Hawk asked on his coms. "We've got two minutes."

"Gotcha loud and clear," she said. Staying behind in the team's van, she volunteered to watch a bank of monitors she gained access to after tapping into the facility's security feeds. She reported that there wasn't any suspicious activity to speak of.

"This all feels too easy," Hawk said.

"Maybe Mrs. Templeton was just messing with us," Black said.

"No," Alex said forcefully. "She wasn't lying. Now, it's possible that Walsh decided to change his mind or Obsidian got cold feet. But I know what I saw—and you saw it too. She was genuinely terrified about what her son might do, not to mention what he'd already done to her."

"Unfortunately, I'm not seeing anything that's giving me a reason to think Walsh is planning on attacking today," Black said. "Just look at this place. It's buttoned up tighter than a camel's ass in a sandstorm."

"Thanks for helping me visualize that one," Alex said. "Without that colorful description, I would've just assumed that terrorists were skipping around like it's recess at an elementary school."

"I've got no metaphors for you," Hawk said, "but I think we may have been played. I'm seeing no movement anywhere nor have I noticed even the slightest bit of suspicious activity. But just keep your eyes peeled."

Hawk scanned around the area once more and noticed NBC correspondent Brittany Tillman making notes on her tablet. She tucked her brown hair behind her ears and looked up as the public address system boomed with an introductory video being broadcast on two giant screens flanking the stage. Holding up her phone, she appeared to be recording the event.

Hawk had watched her short piece on the event the night before as she gushed about the bipartisan effort to create this historic collaborative effort between the country's intelligence agencies. And for someone on the outside like Brittany Tillman, the NSC's creation seemed to be a step in the right direction for keeping the country safe. But Hawk knew better. There were plenty of threats beyond the

U.S. borders, but the more dangerous ones came from within by people who were willing to betray their country for power and money.

The rolling video displayed footage from World War I and II as well as Vietnam and Korea. With a baritone voice, the narrator tugged at the heartstrings of American patriotism.

"When the world needed someone to stand up to powerful dictators, the United States military was up to the task."

From there, the images changed to more cloak and dagger scenes along with footage of the Berlin wall. Then images of terrorist acts, including the toppling of the World Trade Center towers on September 11th.

"Since that time, the theater of war has changed many times, but the brave men and women of this great country have stepped up to answer the call each time."

While bundled up for the Washington winter weather, Hawk still felt the goosebumps on his arms. He couldn't deny the feelings stirred within him as he listened to the emotional narration.

The video came to an abrupt halt as the screen was hijacked by a video espousing a different message. Footage of President Young appeared on the screen of him filmed unknowingly discussing a situation with several foreign ambassadors.

"I know everyone is familiar with the phrase that America doesn't negotiate with terrorists," Young said as he waved his hand dismissively. "But that's just our public message. You bet your ass we're willing to get some of those men home and will do whatever we need to make it happen."

The men sitting with President Young nodded knowingly as the conversation continued.

Hawk heard a murmur roll across the crowd. He glanced at the stage and saw several officials glaring angrily at a man just offstage in the audio/visual booth. He threw his hands in the air in a gesture of surrender, resulting in clenched jaws and fist-shaking from the men standing near the lectern.

"What's going on?" Alex asked. "Everyone looks like they want to charge the stage."

"Someone has seized control of the video screen and is sharing leaked footage of President Young negotiating a backroom deal with the Iranian ambassador," Hawk said.

"Did you know Young did that?" Black asked, joining in the conversation on the coms.

"Absolutely not," Hawk said. "Though I understand why someone might break precedent."

"And for that, I'm thankful," Black said.

"You should be," Alex said. "But we wouldn't

have allowed you to rot in an Al Fatihin prison. We had ulterior motives for negotiating for you."

"Gee, Alex, you know how to make a guy feel special," Black said.

She snickered. "Glad I could boost your esteem."

A dull roar sounded over the speakers when someone yanked the power plug on the video system. But the damning video of President Young had already aired.

"Somebody is gonna get canned for that," Alex said.

"Maybe even some jail time," Black added.

The buzz among the crowd created a distraction, but Hawk maintained his focus. He watched for any sudden movement and noticed a guy who looked like Walsh dressed in a security uniform hustling around the perimeter of the crowd.

"I think I see him," Hawk said. "He's on the southwest corner, wearing an NSC security outfit."

"Are you sure?" Black fired back. "I'm on the northeast side, and I see Walsh."

"Uh, guys," Alex said. "I've found two more men who are spitting images of Walsh."

"So which one is really him?" Black asked. "Alex, can you shed any light on this for us?"

"I'm trying," she said. "I just found Hawk's Walsh and am looking for yours now. I'm running a still shot through NSA's facial recognition program."

"Found him yet?" Black asked. "He's moving away from this area."

"Got him," Alex said. "Just give it a second."

Hawk eased his way through the crowd without drawing any attention. Everyone was still talking about what they'd just seen that they didn't even notice the commotion on the fringes.

"Alex, can you follow me?" Hawk asked. "I'm trailing this one guard who looks just like Walsh."

"I see you," she said. "I'm tagging him right now with the system software. Feel free to go wherever you need to in pursuit of him."

Less than a half minute later, Hawk caught up with the man and grabbed him from behind before spinning him around. The guard fumbled for his gun, but Hawk drew his and told the man to freeze. When Hawk got a clear look at the man, he realized it wasn't Walsh.

"This is a dead end," Hawk said.

"And I suspect all these other men are too," Black said.

"You're right," Alex chimed in. "None of the men are showing up as serious threats in the NSA facial recognition database. So, now what?"

Hawk scanned the front of the new building. He did a double take when he thought he saw something.

252 | R.J. PATTERSON

"Wait a minute," Hawk said. "I see something on the roof."

He broke into a sprint and rounded the corner of the building. He stormed through a side entrance, nearly bowling over a guard who sat on a chair against the wall. He muttered something to Hawk, but he didn't stop.

"You don't have clearance to be in here," the guard shouted with his gun drawn.

"So sue me," Hawk said as he rounded the corner. The man fired a shot, but it had no chance of hitting Hawk, who sprinted up the steps.

"Talk to me, Alex," Hawk said. "Help me get to the roof."

She groaned. "You're on your own this time. I don't have any schematics of the NSC's new building, nor is there any place for me to find them in a reasonable amount of time. You're going to have to rely on your instincts."

Hawk didn't stop climbing the steps until he reached the fifth floor. One more level remained, but there wasn't clear access to it.

"I'm hoping you're seeing something that I'm not," Hawk said.

"Negative," Alex said. "You're going to have to get creative."

Hawk found a hose from an emergency firebox

located near one of the outer offices. Working quickly, he pulled out his knife and sliced through it, making a defacto rope. He hurled a chair against the window and barely avoided the rebound. His second attempt led to some spidered glass as the chair glanced off the side. Hawk picked up the chair a third time, wrapping his fingers around the sides of the back. With one furious throw, the chair shattered the glass, opening a large enough hole for Hawk to work with.

He scrambled over to a chair and used his knife to disassemble the wheelbase before tying it to the end of the hose, which served as a grappling hook. Once Hawk got into position near the window, he hurled his makeshift rope onto the roof. He yanked on it until it held tight before climbing up. When he reached the top, he noticed a man lying prone on the far corner of the building. Hawk drew his gun and raced toward him.

Easing up behind the man, Hawk poked him with his foot.

"I wouldn't move if I were you," Hawk said.

The man didn't move—and then Hawk realized it wasn't a man, but a dummy.

"Dead end," Hawk said, followed by a string of expletives.

"That wasn't him?" Alex asked.

"Just a dummy," Hawk said.

Before Hawk could do anything else, he heard a gunshot rip through the grounds. He ducked down, getting as low as he could until he could figure out what was happening.

"Hawk," Alex said, "that was the real shooter. That was Walsh."

CHAPTER 27

HAWK SURVEYED THE ROOFTOP and noticed another figure on the far side lying prone with a rifle attached to a tripod. The man turned and flashed a grin at Hawk before firing in his direction. Hawk dove to the ground and rolled behind an air conditioning unit in an effort to take cover.

"I found Walsh," Hawk said. "He's atop the southwest corner of the building, shooting from the roof."

Down below, the crowd scattered in a panic. The people on stage crouched low and raced toward safety. Bodyguards swarmed around the government officials to protect them from any more shots.

Hawk leaned around the corner to take a shot at Walsh. He was gone.

"Damn it," Hawk said. "Walsh is on the move. I'm going after him."

"Don't let him get away this time," Alex said. "He just shot Fortner."

"What?" Hawk said as he started to run toward the last spot he saw Walsh.

"Fortner's down," Black said. "I can confirm that. A couple of paramedics are giving him medical attention right now."

"I'm gonna kill that bastard," Hawk said.

"No," Alex said. "We need him alive, Hawk. Don't let your emotions get the best of you."

At that moment, a bullet whizzed right past Hawk's leg. He instinctively dove to the ground.

"What was that?" Hawk asked. "Is there another shooter?"

There was a momentary silence on the coms.

"Alex? Black? Do either of you see anything else?" Hawk asked.

"Wait a minute," Alex said. "I've got the security channel on here. They think you're the one who shot Fortner. There's a shoot-to-kill order out on you, Hawk."

"Please set them straight, Alex."

"I'll do what I can."

Hawk stayed low as he found the rooftop access and descended back into the bowels of the building. He raced down the steps and saw Walsh two flights below.

"I'm still tracking him," Hawk said over the coms. "Alex, watch for where he goes after he exits on the southwest corner of the building."

"Roger that," she said.

Hawk hustled down the steps, skipping two or three at once in order to make up some time.

Moments later, Alex updated Hawk on Walsh's position. "He just turned and went due north."

"Where does it look like he's going?" Hawk asked.

"Straight for the Potomac."

Hawk's lungs burned as he broke into a full sprint outside. In the distance, he could see Walsh, who had a hundred-meter head start. And then, he disappeared into the trees.

"I lost him," Hawk said. "Can you help me out, Alex?"

"I'm tracking him right now using satellite imagery," she said. "He's still heading for the water."

Hawk reached the George Washington Memorial Parkway and darted across the road. He peered through the forestation in the area, looking for any sign of Walsh.

"Alex, I need to know where to go next," Hawk said.

"Keep going," she said. "Once you reach the shore, head south along the bank. He's checking boathouses."

Hawk emerged from the woods and looked

south where a handful of docks dotted the banks of the Potomac River.

"Which one is he at now?" Hawk asked.

"There you are," she said. "Walsh is about two hundred meters away from your position. He just went inside the two-story boathouse. Be careful, Hawk."

Hawk sprinted south, eyeing the location Alex had identified for him. Once he reached the dock leading to the structure, he slowed down and crouched low as he crept toward the door. Right as Hawk approached the entrance, an outboard motor roared to life and a ski boat lurched toward the center of the channel.

Walsh attempted to navigate the boat as he turned back toward Hawk and fired a couple shots. When Walsh returned his focus to steering, Hawk recognized he still had a chance to get onboard by jumping from the dock onto the boat, which was traveling parallel to his position. After racing alongside the vessel, Hawk leaped into the air before crashing hard onto the deck and knocking Walsh forward across the navigational controls. He rolled over into the center of the boat, falling to the floor. Meanwhile, the boat began to spin in a circle.

Hawk reached for his gun, but it must have shaken loose during his landing. Walsh's gun had fallen out of his hand as well and was just out of his reach.

Scrambling toward the weapon, Hawk dove on top of Walsh and tried to reach it first. But Walsh pulled the firearm back with his fingertips before clutching it tightly.

Reacting quickly, Hawk grabbed Walsh's wrist and bashed it against the deck to get him to relinquish his grip. When the gun didn't fall free, Hawk tried to hold Walsh's arm in place while punching him in the throat. But Walsh twisted to avoid a devastating blow as the two men rose to their feet while wrestling for the weapon.

After a brief struggle, Hawk moved into a more advantageous position, leaning on Walsh as his back was pinned against the edge of the boat and arms were fully extended arms over the water. The vessel continued to spin in a circle, unsteadying Hawk's balance. He decided to make another lunge for the weapon. And when he did, it finally came loose from Walsh's hand before tumbling into the Potomac.

Stunned for a moment by the disappearance of the weapon, Hawk was caught off guard when Walsh used both feet to shove Hawk backward, nearly knocking him into the water. Walsh scrambled behind the steering wheel and pulled the boat out of its spin. Hawk regained his composure and took a flying leap at Walsh, diving over the windshield and toppling him to the ground. The boat veered toward the far shore and ran around a few seconds later while the two men fought.

Walsh seized his chance to escape, jumping out of the vessel and running onto the shore. Hawk followed Walsh along the bank until they reached an inlet that ran up against a nature trail surrounded by a canal on one side and the Potomac on the other. Walsh was fighting his way through bushes and brambles when Hawk made a run at the Obsidian agent.

Walsh spun around and grabbed a knife from his ankle holster and waved it at Hawk.

"You ready to die just like your mother did?" Walsh asked.

Rage coursed through Hawk's veins.

"Hawk, I lost visual contact with you, but I wanted to let you know that a whole host of law enforcement agents are closing in on your position," Alex said over the coms.

"So am I," Black said.

Hawk narrowed his eyes and glared at Walsh.

"So, you are ready to die like her?" Walsh said. He gestured with his hand, bidding for Hawk to come closer.

"We're going to end this right now," Hawk said.

CHAPTER 28

HAWK LOOKED AROUND for something he could use to fend off Walsh. A large branch a few feet away had to suffice as Hawk realized he was running out of options—and time. While diving back into the Potomac would help him avoid Walsh, Hawk would be apprehended by the security detail rushing toward his location.

"My contact told me you'd be difficult to eliminate," Walsh said. "But this is going to be easier than I thought."

"Yet you didn't kill me in New Mexico when you had a chance," Hawk said.

"I didn't realize my own mother would set a trap for me."

"A trap? It's more like she set one for us."

Walsh shook his head. "Is that why she only told me about you and the woman agent? I could've handled both of you, but she didn't tell me about the third person. I would've brought some help. I just had to save myself at that point."

"So instead you shot your own mother?" Hawk asked.

"I was doing her a favor. She was about to be arrested by the FBI for human trafficking and smuggling. It's not like she was some paragon of virtue. Besides, she's the one who made me murder all her husbands for her because she couldn't bring herself to do it."

"You don't have to choose this path," Hawk said. "You can lay down your weapon, and you can help us stop Obsidian."

Walsh laughed. "You're never gonna stop them."

"I won't if I don't know who's behind all this. But you do—and you could assist us in bringing the leaders to justice."

"Justice? These people own the justice system and everything else."

"They don't own me."

"They will," Walsh said. "Just give Obsidian time."

"I won't be co-opted by anyone. That's not how I operate."

"It won't matter. You'll be their slave one way or another—unless you want to fight this. I'll give you a quick out, probably even your best solution."

"Never," Hawk sneered.

He ran straight for Walsh before darting to the side just before reaching him. Hawk avoided Walsh's blade and then swung the branch at his knee. As Hawk made contact, Walsh let out a scream as a cracking sound ripped through the air. Hawk tumbled on the ground before jumping back to his feet.

Walsh grimaced as he regained his balance then turned to face Hawk.

"None of this is going to matter when the event happens," Walsh said.

"The event? What was today?"

"Merely the pre-cursor to what's about to unfold all across the world," Walsh said. "Obsidian is about to assume control, the likes of which this world has never seen in the modern age. You think communism was bad? Wait until you see what they're going to do."

Hawk shook his head. "Yet you stand by them and fight for them."

"It's how I'm going to survive—and why you're about to die."

Hawk motioned for Walsh to come toward him. "I'm not going anywhere."

Walsh lunged toward Hawk and swiped at him. The blade slashed Hawk's bicep, drawing some blood. But it wasn't enough to make him wince as he swung back with the branch.

Hawk hit the top of Walsh's hand, forcing him

to release the knife. Both men dove for the weapon that fell into a nearby bush. Hawk got his fingers on the edge of the grip, but Walsh snatched it away and rolled on top of Hawk.

"It's over," Walsh said.

He reared back and prepared to plunge the blade into Hawk's chest when a bullet ripped through Walsh's chest. He dropped the knife as he clutched the gaping wound on his right side with both hands.

Alertly, Hawk grabbed the knife and watched as Walsh fell onto his back and gasped for air.

"You're right," Hawk said. "It's over."

A boat roared up near them on the shore.

"Please drop your weapon immediately and place your hands where we can see them," ordered an officer over the boat's speaker.

Hawk flung the knife a healthy distance away before taking Walsh's phone and then raising both hands in the air. He looked down at Walsh, who was still struggling to breathe.

"My phone won't help you," Walsh whispered. "You better run. You'll never get out of prison alive, if they don't shoot you on-site."

Walsh closed his eyes and ceased breathing as he fell limp. Hawk sighed before slowly rising to his feet.

A couple officers stormed toward Hawk.

"Keep your hands where I can see them," one of

the men said.

Hawk didn't move as they searched him for a weapon. After a quick check, one of the guards announced that Hawk was clean. "But there's a dead body over here."

"Two of you stay behind here while we send for another boat," one of the men on the vessel said. "Let's take him back to NSC headquarters and process him there. Everyone is gonna want their pound of flesh from this clown."

Black darted through the woods and approached the officers with his hands in the air. "It's okay," Black said, slowly reaching to hold up the badge attached to a chain around his neck. "I'm Special Agent Grant with the bureau. This man is a hero, not a criminal. He's the one who apprehended the actual suspect."

The man in charge huffed. "We're handling this now. You can take that up with all the eyewitnesses who reported something to the contrary. Now, if you'll excuse us, we need to process this traitor."

Glancing at Black, Hawk cut his eyes toward his front right pocket. "Get my phone and call my lawyer. I'm sure he'll be able to sort out this misunderstanding. And thanks."

Black nodded before he fished the phone out of Hawk's pants amid protests from the officers.

"Rob Fulchum is my lawyer," Hawk said. "He'll

know what to do."

As the men escorted Hawk to the boat, they eyed Black closely.

"Come on, guys," Black pleaded. "Let me contact his lawyer for him. You're going to be embarrassed about arresting him when the footage comes out."

"Whatever," one of the guards replied. "Call his lawyer for him. It's not gonna make much difference. He shot Fortner, who's in the hospital fighting for his life."

CHAPTER 29

ALEX TOOK THE PHONE from Black and gained access to it by generating a simulated fingerprint she found on file from Mack Walsh. She downloaded all of the data onto her computer and started to comb through it while listening to radio reports about what the security detail believed happened.

"Thanks," Alex said. "I know what you did out there. If you hadn't shot Walsh when you did . . ."

"Just doing my job," Black said. "We've all got each other's back around here. Let's just hope Blunt can get everything cleared up soon."

Black studied the video monitors depicting certain sections around the new NSC campus. Investigators collected casings, while paramedics continued to check attendees for any injuries.

"I would've sworn that I saw Walsh on the ground," Black said.

"Those look-alikes threw everything off," Alex said. "And I can't figure out where they went."

Black nodded knowingly. "Look, I know we're all focused on getting this information off Walsh's phone, but I can't imagine what you're going through right now."

"I'm trying not to think about it," Alex said. "I do take some solace in the fact that President Young is an ally of ours and the Phoenix Foundation. But now that we've had time to catch our breath and reflect, this whole scenario felt like a setup. Obsidian wanted Hawk here so they could frame him."

"What makes you so sure of that?"

"Somebody on the inside had knowledge of where all the security cameras were," Alex said. "This building is brand new, and somehow Walsh avoided being seen. We know that Hawk saw him because he chased him across the river. But no one else did apparently, at least if the chatter I hear on the law enforcement communications is to be believed."

"But why?" Black asked. "If Obsidian wanted Hawk dead, they had their chances."

"There's something else at play here," Alex said. "It's almost as if they wanted to prove something with this attack. I haven't sorted through all potential reasons why yet, but it seems as though a brazen act of this nature could trigger something else they wanted. And framing Hawk would help further that agenda."

"So to thwart this, all we have to do now is prove Hawk's innocence."

"Easier said than done, and I'm not sure how to do it," Alex said. "But I do know the FBI investigators are confused as to how Hawk was seen running from one side of the rooftop to the other without a weapon, but there were long-range shots fired from both locations. I also heard someone say that there were no prints on the weapon that was positioned next to a dummy."

"Of course," Black said. "A dummy's not gonna leave prints."

"But the working theory is that Hawk was shooting from both locations."

Black shook his head emphatically. "There's no way this sticks. Have you spoken with Blunt yet?"

"I have no idea where is he. In the midst of all this chaos, he could've been taken to the hospital, but I haven't heard from him."

"I'll try to reach him," Black said. "You just keep working on Walsh's phone."

* * *

BLACK STEPPED OUTSIDE the van and dialed Blunt's number. The call went straight to voicemail.

He sighed and meandered toward the stage where an FBI forensics team worked to gather every shred of evidence. On the rooftop, Black spied a pair of suits strolling around and pointing at something on the ground.

Black contemplated his next move. The only silver bullet he had remaining in his chamber was to call the president. While Alex touted her relationship with him, Black knew President Young as well, executing several secret assignments for him when it came to gathering intelligence on his political rivals. Although hesitant to comply with the president's requests, Black figured it might be able to earn him some political capital in the future. And if there was ever a moment to call in a favor, it was now.

Black called the president's secretary and left a message. Two minutes later, Black's phone buzzed.

"Please hold for the president," a woman said. Seconds later, President Young joined the line.

"Titus, how the hell are ya?" Young asked.

"To be completely honest and get straight to the point, I'd be better if I wasn't standing here watching this disaster unfold at the NSC dedication."

"I was hoping you weren't calling about that. My office is already trying to do damage control over that leaked footage someone broadcast during the introduction while hijacking the video system."

"Well, it's a lot worse for Brady Hawk," Black said.

"Brady's in trouble?"

"He's been arrested as the shooter who fired on the stage."

"That's absurd."

"Of course it is," Black said. "But it's pretty apparent this was an elaborate setup job by Obsidian."

"This is getting out of control. If anything, we need Brady out there more than ever to track these people down, whoever they are."

"I agree, sir. And the worst thing is we were making some progress, but the man behind the plot is now dead."

"So Brady is just twisting in the wind right now?" Young asked.

"Unless you do something about it, he's going to be in serious trouble. Even worse is that his cover might be blown if this gets leaked to the media."

Young sighed. "I'm afraid right now that there isn't anything I can do to help him."

"Of course there is, sir. You can order the FBI to release him and make all record of his detainment vanish. All you have to do is pick up the phone."

"Not now, not after the world just found out we actually negotiate with terrorists on occasion. Just think of how it would look if I wielded my influence now. It'd seem like I was trying to manipulate the situation for my advantage. That's not politically expedient for me right now."

"Are there any other backchannels we can work right now?" Black asked.

"I would suggest calling Fortner, but he's not going to be of any help to you since he's in a coma."

Black shook his head. "I hadn't heard that. I just knew that he had been hit and was going to the hospital."

"It's touch-and-go if he's going to make it through the night."

"This is really bad," Black said.

"Your best bet is to prove his innocence and find a way to do that quickly."

"Will do, sir. Thanks for your time."

"Of course. I'll be watching," Young said before he hung up.

Black let out an exasperated breath as he looked skyward. He circled the area around the stage before wandering toward a bank of media vehicles, many of them with correspondents reporting with the investigation unfolding right behind them. He watched NBC's Brittany Tillman wrap up her segment before dropping her mic and staring intently at her iPad. Sauntering up to her, he asked her what she saw.

She furrowed her brow. "Are you taking an official statement from me? Because someone else already did that."

Black offered his hand. "Special Agent Grant."

"Brittany Tillman on special assignment," she said with a faint smile. "I was supposed to fly out of here tonight to the Dominican for my best friend's wedding. But I'm stuck here for now."

"Stuck?" he asked.

"Yeah, they're not letting anyone leave, not that it'd matter. My editor isn't about to let me leave this place until I have the real story about what's going on. Any chance you can help me with that?"

Black shrugged. "Maybe. Depends on what you know."

"Well, I don't know much other than what we're getting from media releases on social media. However, I do have some interesting footage of my own."

Black's eyes widened. "What kind of footage?"

"I just started filming on my tablet when the initial video began. I wanted to get a wide shot for my own personal records, so I set the device down and started making a few notes when the takeover of the video system occurred."

"Can I see it?" Black asked.

"Sure, I guess," she said. After entering the password, she opened up the footage and started playing the clip. Black moved the video along to the moment just before the shooting began.

"Would you look at that?" he said before his mouth fell agape.

"What is it?" Brittany asked.

"Look on top of the building about thirty seconds before the shooting begins."

She watched the man on top moving around and then disappearing just before the first shots were fired.

"What was I looking at there?" she asked.

"Back it up and look on the other side of the roof," Black suggested.

When she did, she put her hand on her mouth and then shot a glance at Black.

"The man on the right just running around without a long-range gun, he's one of the good guys," Black said. "He's the one who's being accused of staging this entire attack."

"And the man on the left?"

"That's Mack Walsh, a man who murdered a federal judge about ten years ago and has been wanted by the FBI ever since."

"And they arrested the man on the right?" she asked.

Black nodded. "He's an undercover agent. Please blur his face before you put this out there so no one can see who he is. It's a matter of national security."

She knit her brow. "You're not going to confiscate this from me?"

"I'd love a copy," he said, "but in light of all that happened today, I think it'd be best if this story were debunked by someone other than a law enforcement agency and merely confirmed by them. Plus, it's going to make your career and win you some kind of reporting award."

She smiled. "Are you sure there's no catch?"

"None," he said with a wink. "I'm just trying to help a friend."

Black gave Brittany an email address to send the footage to, and by the time he returned to the van, he already had it.

"Did President Young help?" Alex asked as Black strode into the van.

Black shook his head. "But don't fret. I've got something even better."

She sighed, her eyes welling up with tears. "It better be good."

"Watch this," Black said as he started the footage and held his phone out so Alex could see it. Once she noticed there were two men on the roof, she zoomed in on Walsh. That's it. This will exonerate Hawk."

"No doubt about it," Black said. "I just need to get this into the hands of the agent in charge of the case."

"Great work," she said. "He'll be forever indebted to you for getting this footage."

"Too late for that," Black said. "He already owes me for shooting Walsh just as he was about to stab

Hawk. I'm gonna have to figure out a way to cash in on all these things Hawk owes me for."

"I'm sure he'll balance the ledger at some point soon," she said. "By the way, have you heard back from Blunt yet?"

"Still no word," Black said. "I'm starting to get concerned."

"If you're concerned about that, wait until you hear what I found on Walsh's phone."

CHAPTER 30

HAWK WAS RELEASED FROM FBI custody later that evening after giving his full statement to the bureau. He greeted Alex with a long embrace before shaking Black's hand and giving him a quick side hug. Blunt, who had been stuck going over hours of interviews with several agency directors following the attack, waited back against the wall and smiled at his trio of agents.

"You look like a proud father," Alex said to Blunt, who was working on another unlit cigar.

"Perhaps that's because it's exactly how I feel," he said. "You were incredible today, diffusing what could've been an even more disastrous situation and working quickly on the fly to prove Hawk's innocence. It's why you're all the best at what you do."

"We haven't done anything yet," Black said.

Blunt nodded. "So I've been told. Is it too soon to talk about this at the office?"

"As long as you buy us plenty of food and drinks,

we'll talk all night long," Hawk said.

"I'll make it happen," he said. "I'll meet you back at the office in an hour."

* * *

HAWK INSISTED on stopping back by his apartment with Alex to take a quick shower and get a fresh change of clothes. Swimming in the Potomac River resulted in a pungent odor settling everywhere. Alex admitted that she didn't care what he smelled like as long as he was alive, drawing a hearty laugh from Hawk.

"Not everyone will feel the same way as you," Hawk said.

When they reached the office, they took their seats as Blunt and Black were already sitting down and waiting.

Blunt removed the cigar out of his mouth and studied the chewed end for a moment before jamming it back between his teeth. He swirled some bourbon around in his glass and then took a long swig, draining all the contents.

"It's been that kind of day," Blunt said as he placed the tumbler down hard on the tabletop.

"It's been that kind of week," Black said as he poured himself a drink.

"It's been that kind of month," Hawk added, "or maybe even year. Tracking Obsidian has been like chasing a ghost."

Alex chimed in. "The only difference is we know this ghost is real."

"So catch me up to speed on everything," Blunt said.

"Before we do that," Alex said, "I'd like to hear an update on Fortner. Do you know if he's going to pull through?"

"I was told Fortner was in a coma," Blunt said. "I went to the hospital where they took him following the incident and tried to get in to see him, but I was denied access. One of the doctors told me that they were uncertain if he'd make through the night. However, something didn't seem right to me."

"What do you mean?" Hawk asked.

"I just had a feeling that the doc was feeding me some bullshit," Blunt said. "So, I asked one of the nurses about Fortner. She told me that he had been moved hours ago. Yet there were still several agents posted outside the door."

"Why would they still be there if Fortner was gone?" Alex asked.

"That's exactly what I want to know," Blunt said.

"Well, maybe I can help shed some light on that for you," she said.

"You were able to crack open Walsh's phone?" he asked.

She nodded. "It's not as difficult as you think, so don't throw me any parades just yet."

"I love you, honey," Hawk said, "but if anyone is getting a parade around here, it's Black. He saved my life twice today, once with his spectacular shooting skills and the other with his detective prowess."

Black waved off Hawk dismissively. "One of those was luck."

"Luck or skill—it doesn't matter to me," Hawk said. "I'm here right now because of what you did in both situations."

Alex sighed. "You can sleep on the couch tonight," she said with a wry grin.

"As long as it's not a jail cell, I don't care," Hawk said with a wink.

"Anyway, as I was about to say earlier," she continued, "Walsh's phone proved to be quite the treasure trove for us. The fact that it wasn't more heavily encrypted underscores just how arrogant he was. I'm pretty sure he thought he was going to frame Hawk and get away without being caught."

"What kind of information did you find that backs that up?" Blunt asked.

"There are several text message threads from different numbers, indicating that either Obsidian leadership is exercising extreme caution by changing phones every few days or that there are several people who were directing Walsh. Either way, it raises some serious questions."

"Were you able to find out where those calls originated from?" Hawk asked.

"Of course," she said. "I cross-checked them with data gathered from the NSA and found that they were in various parts of the city, except for one number. It was recorded as 'not available', which means it was from someone inside one of our intelligence agencies as that's how calls in those sectors are classified when recorded."

"It was one of our own?" Blunt asked.

"Every time we encountered Walsh, he warned us that Obsidian is operated by powerful people and that we don't have any idea just how powerful they are," Alex said. "I just ignored these inane statements for the most part until I came across a file of deleted voicemails. They were supposedly removed from the phone, but I know how to retrieve them."

Blunt narrowed his eyes. "You have the perpetrator's voice?"

"Sort of," Alex said. "Listen to this." She pushed the play button on a recovered message.

"You need to eliminate Brady Hawk," a man said in a heavily modulated voice. "He needs to be framed for an attempted assassination. I will send you details on how to make that happen."

The team all stared at one another with raised eyebrows and mouths agape.

"We don't know who that is?" Black asked.

Alex put her finger in the air. "I was able to reverse engineer the modulation and come up with what the person actually sounds like. Here it is."

The recording played again, this time without all the extra effects. When it finished, Blunt buried his face in his hands and sighed.

"I never would've guessed that," he said.

"Walsh was right," Hawk said. "There are far more powerful people than we ever could've imagined pulling the strings behind Obsidian."

Blunt nodded in agreement. "Yes, but I never would've guessed that General Fortner would've been one of them."

"But that's not all," Alex said. "I found another deleted voicemail and didn't immediately recognize the voice. So, I put it into the NSA's system and cross-checked it against their audio database."

"Anyone we know?" Black asked.

"Tanya Starikov, the Russian billionairess who owns Sermo, the fastest-growing social media platform on the planet," Alex said.

"How come I've never heard of it?" Blunt asked.

Alex chuckled. "The fact that you've never heard of a trendy social media company doesn't surprise me.

However, you'll get a pass on this one since its users are primarily in Europe, Asia, and Africa. But they're expanding here soon."

"And she's working in conjunction with Fortner?" Blunt asked. "That seems rather unlikely."

Alex shrugged. "He's probably working for her."

"Now what?" Black asked.

"You and Hawk are going infiltrate Sermo."

Blunt's phone buzzed with a call. He glanced at the screen. "I better take this."

* * *

BLUNT STOOD AND LUMBERED out of the room before accepting the call.

"Please stay on the line for the President of the United States," a woman's voice said.

After a few clicks, Noah Young's smooth voice came through. "J.D., are you okay?"

"I've been better, but I'm alive. What about you?" Blunt said.

"Just trying to fend off this PR nightmare."

"I wish I could help you, sir, but that's not exactly my strong suit."

"You owe me one after that stunt you pulled going around me and Fortner to get Agent Black back home."

Blunt remained silent.

"What? You didn't think I was going to find out

about that?" Young asked.

"I'm sorry, sir. I couldn't just leave one of my men out there, and I couldn't exactly get help from anyone to retrieve him either since we don't really do what we're doing."

"I understand why you did it and I'm glad it worked out for you, but you still usurped my authority. It's bad enough that I once said that I'd negotiate with terrorists, even though I never did. But if this ever came to light that what I said was more than a statement taken out of context, the press—and any future political candidates I face—will eat me alive."

"So what do you need, Mr. President? Just name it."

"I need a win right now, and we just received some intelligence about Al Fatihin and what they're planning," Young said. "I need you to capture Evana Bahar within the next month."

"That's a tall order, sir. You remember how long it took us to catch Karif Fazil?"

"I wouldn't ask if I didn't think you could deliver."

"But there are other problems we're dealing with now and—"

"Nothing is bigger than this one," Young said. "I think you know if I go down, the Phoenix Foundation is going to crumble into ashes and never arise again."

Blunt sighed. "Okay, we'll get on it, sir. I'm meeting with the team right now."

"Thank you, J.D. You're a great American."

Blunt hung up and returned to the conference room.

"Was that President Young?" Alex asked.

"It was," Blunt said. "And he's got a different assignment for us."

"There's nothing more important than stopping Obsidian right now," Hawk said.

"That's not how President Young sees it. We owe him—and he wants us to catch Evana Bahar."

Hawk nodded. "Well, in that case, it'd be my pleasure to accept this assignment."

"And he wants it done within a month," Blunt added.

"Well," Hawk said, "I guess we better quit fretting over Obsidian and start making plans to take out Evana Bahar."

THE END

ACKNOWLEDGMENTS

I am grateful to so many people who have helped with the creation of this project and the entire Brady Hawk series.

Krystal Wade was a big help in editing this book as always.

I would also like to thank my advance reader team for all their input in improving this book along with all the other readers who have enthusiastically embraced the story of Brady Hawk. Stay tuned ... there's more Brady Hawk coming soon.

ABOUT THE AUTHOR

R.J. PATTERSON is an award-winning writer living in southeastern Idaho. He first began his illustrious writing career as a sports journalist, recording his exploits on the soccer fields in England as a young boy. Then when his father told him that people would pay him to watch sports if he would write about what he saw, he went all in. He landed his first writing job at age 15 as a sports writer for a daily newspaper in Orangeburg, S.C. He later attended earned a degree in newspaper journalism from the University of Georgia, where he took a job covering high school sports for the award-winning *Athens Banner-Herald* and *Daily News*.

He later became the sports editor of *The Valdosta Daily Times* before working in the magazine world as an editor and freelance journalist. He has won numerous writing awards, including a national award for his investigative reporting on a sordid tale surrounding an NCAA investigation over the University of Georgia football program.

R.J. enjoys the great outdoors of the Northwest while living there with his wife and four children. He still follows sports closely. He also loves connecting with readers and would love to hear from you. To stay updated about future projects, connect with him over Facebook or on the interwebs at www.RJPbooks.com and sign up for his newsletter to get deals and updates.

Made in United States
Troutdale, OR
04/26/2024

19463439R00181